The SECRET GARDEN COOKBOOK

The
SECRET
GARDEN
COOKBOOK

RECIPES INSPIRED BY FRANCES HODGSON BURNETT'S

The Secret Garden

AMY COTLER

illustrations by Prudence See

■ HarperCollins*Publishers*

Thanks to my dad, who taught me to love looking it up, whatever
it was; my editor, Alix Reid, who kept me on course; and
my husband, who is forever cheerful about
the odd array of food on the table.

Excerpts from *The Secret Garden* by Frances Hodgson Burnett

The Secret Garden Cookbook
Text copyright © 1999 by Amy Cotler
Illustrations copyright © 1999 by Prudence See
Printed in the U.S.A. All rights reserved.
http://www.harperchildrens.com

Library of Congress Cataloging-in-Publication Data
Cotler, Amy.
    The secret garden cookbook : recipes inspired by Frances Hodgson Burnett's The
secret garden / Amy Cotler ; illustrations by Prudence See.
        p.   cm.
    Includes index.
    Summary: A compilation of recipes for foods served in England during the Victorian
Era and inspired by characters and events in "The Secret Garden" by Frances Hodgson
Burnett.
    ISBN 0-06-027740-8
    1. Cookery, English—Juvenile literature.   2. Food habits—England—History—19th
century—Juvenile literature.   [1. Cookery, English.   2. Food habits—England—History.
3. Literary cookbooks.]   I. See, Prudence, ill.   II. Burnett, Frances Hodgson, 1849–1924.
Secret garden.   III. Title.
TX717.C588   1999   98-22437
394.1'0942—dc21   CIP
                                                                                      AC

1   2   3   4   5   6   7   8   9   10
❖
First Edition

To the magic in The Secret Garden,
to the magic in my daughter, Emma, and
to our bedtime reading together

—*A.C.*

AUTHOR'S NOTE

Heat burns Victorian and modern children alike.

So when cooking these recipes,

kindly use caution and, where necessary,

work with an adult to help you out.

Table of Contents

The Secret Garden and the Magic of Food 10

Yorkshire Breakfasts 15
Porridge 18
Coddled Eggs 20
Cheese Muffins 22
Little Sausage Cakes 24
Cocoa 26

A Manor Lunch 29
Yorkshire Pudding 32
Roasted Fowl with Bread Sauce 34
Potato Snow 36
Welsh Rabbit 38
Cabinet Pudding 40
Jam Roly Poly 42

An English Tea 45
A Proper Pot of Tea 48
Cucumber Tea Sandwiches 50
Scones 52
Fruit Tea Loaf 54
Lemon Curd Tartlettes 56
Brandy Snap Baskets with Whipped Cream 58

The Kitchen Garden 61
Fresh Spring Peas with Mint 64
Glazed Carrots 66

Summer Pudding 68
Two Fools 70
Raspberry Jam 72
Raspberry Vinegar 74
Molded Spiced Pears 76
Strawberries and Cream 78

Dickon's Cottage Food 81

Tattie Broth 84
Pease Pudding 86
Yorkshire Oatcakes 88
Cottage Loaf 90
Dough–Cakes with Brown Sugar 92
Parkin 94

A Taste of India 97

Fruit Lassi 100
Sooji 102
Little Bacon and Coriander Pancakes 104
Fresh Mango Chutney 106
Mulligatawny Soup 108
Florence Nightingale's Kedgeree 110

Garden Picnics 113

Roasted Potatoes and Eggs 116
Currant Buns 118
Crumpets 120
Cornish Pasties 122
Chocolate Picnic Biscuits 124

Index 126

The
SECRET
GARDEN
COOKBOOK

The Secret Garden and the Magic of Food

Mary

Mary was glowing with exercise and good spirits.

"I'm getting fatter and fatter every day," she said quite exultantly.

"Mrs. Medlock will have to get me some bigger dresses. Martha says my hair is growing thicker. It isn't so flat and stringy."

—The Secret Garden
Chapter 16

Frances Hodgson Burnett's *The Secret Garden* is about the magic of making things come alive. Mary, Colin, and Dickon all help the forgotten secret garden to grow again. But Mary and Colin come alive too, through hard work, friendship, and good nourishing food.

When Mary Lennox first arrives at Misselthwaite Manor from India, she is thin, sallow, and unhealthy-looking. But as she goes outside, skips rope, and works in the garden, her appetite grows. Colin, too, is sickly, until he learns the secret of the garden. By the end of the novel he is enjoying food as much as Mary. Pails of fresh milk, dough-cakes with brown sugar, hearty porridge, fire-roasted potatoes—Mary and Colin can't get enough of them!

The children of *The Secret Garden* grew up during the reign of Queen Victoria, who ruled from 1837 to 1901—so long that her reign became commonly known as the Victorian Era. During this time there were those who pleaded to abolish her position, because the monarchy cost the nation a lot of money while many English people went hungry. By the last half of her reign, though, Queen Victoria herself became quite popular. She was titled Empress of India in 1876, and her golden jubilee in 1887, which marked her fiftieth year as Queen, was a national celebration.

In those days food took a long time to cook and serve. Thus, even households that did not have a lot of money employed one or more servants to cook meals, as having a cook saved a great deal of time.

While food was time-consuming to prepare, it was also often fresher than it is today, at least for those who had access to vegetable and fruit gardens. All the children in *The Secret Garden* lived primarily on food grown close to home in kitchen gardens. Misselthwaite had a large kitchen garden, and most likely a greenhouse for out-of-season produce. These would have been attended to by several servants: the head gardener, Mr. Roach, and his undergardener, Mr. Weatherstaff. In addition, the manor probably raised chickens and dairy cows, or purchased fresh poultry and milk from local farmers.

Wealthy children like Mary and Colin were well fed and had a wide variety of meats, dairy products, and vegetables to chose from. By contrast, poorer children often went hungry. Dickon's family, which lived a few miles away from Misselthwaite, was crowded into a tiny four-room cottage. With fourteen hungry mouths to feed, there often wasn't enough to go around, and what

Colin

"I think we shall have to eat it all this morning, Mary," Colin always ended by saying. *"We can send away some of the lunch and a great deal of the dinner."*
But they never found they could send away anything. . . .
"I do wish," Colin would say also, *"I do wish the slices of ham were thicker, and one muffin each is not enough for any one."*
—The Secret Garden
Chapter 24

there was was never wasted. This is why Martha was so shocked when Mary refused to eat her porridge! Luckily, like many country folk, Dickon's family was able to supplement the simple and scanty diet of oatmeal and bread with whatever Dickon could grow in the garden, such as potatoes, turnips, and carrots.

Despite the almost fairy-tale-like feeling in *The Secret Garden*, nineteenth-century England was in a period of great turmoil and poverty and hunger and change. The country's population grew to four times its size, so there were thousands of new mouths to feed. Many of these new mouths belonged to children, who were forced to leave the land and move to industrial towns to look for ways to earn a living. There they worked long hours in factories, which were springing up all over the place. They had no access to fresh vegetables, fresh milk, or fresh meat; sometimes they could not find fresh water to drink. Often their only meals were bread and jam.

Perhaps because of this time of great change and great hunger, Burnett imagined a world in which everyone has access to fresh food—and plenty of it. Even Mrs. Sowerby, Dickon's mother, though she must feed fourteen, manages to find a little extra food for Mary and Colin when they experience the joys of eating.

In her book, Burnett celebrates the wonders of good

appetite, good food, and good health. I hope that this cookbook, with recipes inspired by the foods and culture in *The Secret Garden*, will pay tribute to Burnett, as well as providing an antidote to our own age, when more often than not we disdain those with good appetites and a hearty appreciation of good food.

Martha

"Eh! you should see 'em all," Martha said. *"There's twelve of us an' my father only gets sixteen shilling a week. I can tell you my mother's put to it to get porridge for 'em all. They tumble about on th' moor an' play there all day an' mother says th' air of th' moor fattens 'em. She says she believes they eat th' grass same as th' wild ponies do."*

—The Secret Garden
Chapter 4

After a few days spent almost entirely out of doors Mary wakened one morning knowing what it was to be hungry, and when she sat down to her breakfast she did not glance disdainfully at her porridge and push it away, but took up her spoon and began to eat it and went on eating it until her bowl was empty.

"Tha' got on well enough with that this mornin', didn't tha'?" said Martha.

"It tastes nice today," said Mary, feeling a little surprised herself.

"It's th' air of th' moor that's givin' thee stomach for tha' victuals," answered Martha.

—The Secret Garden
Chapter 5

Yorkshire Breakfasts

Porridge

Coddled Eggs

Cheese Muffins

Little Sausage Cakes

Cocoa

Yorkshire

The primary setting of The Secret Garden *is the moors of Yorkshire, England's largest shire, or county. But Yorkshire isn't only moorland. It also has an industrial southwest region, in which wool from hearty moorland sheep is processed. The rest of Yorkshire's 4 million acres is divided between lush pastureland and moor. Today, ancient moorland towns still have altars and stones, as well as bowls and pottery left by dwellers who lived there 2,000 years ago!*

Yorkshire Breakfasts

Just as Mary, Dickon, and Colin are characters in *The Secret Garden*, so too is Yorkshire, located in the north of England. In the beginning of the story, when Mary's carriage first pulls her across the Yorkshire moor, the land appears endless, bleak, and desolate. In fact, though, the moors are covered with low-lying shrubs, such as heather, that bloom a carpet of purple in the summer, and bilberries, that are a lot like our blueberries. They are also inhabited by a menagerie of wild animals, such as the ponies and foxes and rabbits that Dickon befriends.

The agricultural roots of Yorkshire shape its simple but hearty country food, food that Colin and Mary learn to love. The rustic fare of Yorkshire is the perfect match for the raw, damp weather of northern England. It is plain, but filling enough to fortify farmers who labored in fields and pastures tending sheep, and the children, like Mary, Colin, and Dickon, who played in the strong moorland wind.

Cottage children (who were so called because they lived in small stone cottages) like Dickon and his eleven siblings gobbled up large bowls of cheap but filling porridge for their morning meal. Porridge was also a part of manor children's breakfast. However, in a manor house like Misselthwaite, meals were generally an elaborate affair, with many dishes accompanying the porridge.

A typical breakfast for a household like Misselthwaite Manor might start with the footman sounding a gong at eight or nine o'clock to notify family and staff to assemble in the morning room. After prayers, most of the servants were dismissed and the family was seated. The footman brought in breakfast, the mistress of the house poured tea, and her eldest daughter or the lady to her right poured coffee. When everyone was served, the footman and the butler withdrew.

A Yorkshire breakfast almost always included eggs and bacon, served in a wide variety of ways. To break up the monotony of this daily diet, though, other dishes were introduced, often utilizing bits of whatever was left over from the night before. Meat hashes, relatives of the familiar corned-beef hash, were commonly made with the remains of a joint, commonly mutton. As many as three additional meat dishes might be served as well, including glazed sheeps' tongues, mutton chops, kidneys, and fried rabbit! Toast and "fancy breads," such as muffins, crumpets, and scones, also accompanied these breakfasts. Favorite breakfast drinks were coffee, tea, and chocolate. Fortunately for Mary and Colin, chocolate at breakfast was favored for children over tea, as it was thought to be more nutritious.

The Moors

Robin Hood, Captain Cook, James Herriot, and the Brontë sisters were all from Yorkshire. Emily Brontë made famous the howling sound the wind makes as it sweeps across the treeless moor in her book Wuthering Heights. *"Wuthering" was the word Brontë used to describe this mournful sound. Martha described the sound "as if some one was lost on th' moor an' wailin'."*

Porridge

Porridge, which is made of boiled oats and is also called oatmeal, was considered an extremely healthy breakfast, and children of all classes ate it regularly for breakfast. Eaten hot or cold, it was nourishing, filling, and inexpensive to make. Wealthy children often ate porridge with sugar and cream, while poorer children ate it with skimmed milk and treacle (English molasses) or salt. Mary wasn't used to eating such a filling breakfast, but the hearty Yorkshire air soon gave her a good appetite.

Ingredients

1 cup water
¾ cup old-fashioned rolled oats
pinch of salt
2 tablespoons currants or raisins (optional)
pinch of cinnamon (optional)
pinch of nutmeg (optional)

Procedure

1. Put the water into a small pot and bring it to a rapid boil. Stir in the oats, salt, and if you are using them, currants or raisins, and cinnamon and nutmeg.

2. Reduce the heat to a simmer and cook, uncovered, for 10 minutes.

3. Serve hot in bowls, topped with brown sugar and milk to taste.

Makes 2 servings.

A stalk of oats

How to Enhance Your Appetite for Breakfast

Early in The Secret Garden, *Mary had trouble working up a healthy appetite. Apparently a lack of morning appetite was not unusual. Period medical handbooks list cures for those not hungry in the morning. One suggests a wife insist that her husband take an "air bath" when he has no morning appetite. What's an air bath? You had to remove your clothes outside in the morning air, then rub yourself down with a rough sponge, also called a loofah!*

Cook

Coddled Eggs

Although not always easy to find in the city, eggs were considered an essential breakfast dish in the country. To break up the monotony of eggs every day, eggs were served in a multitude of styles. Eggs cooked in a cup, or "coddled," made a comforting breakfast. As Mary gained a healthy appetite, she might have enjoyed these eggs, along with buttered toast and little sausage cakes, before running outside to meet Dickon in the secret garden.

For a variation on this recipe, after you break the eggs into their cups, sprinkle each with a teaspoon of finely chopped tomato or cooked bacon, or, when the egg is cooked, a teaspoon of your favorite cheese, finely grated.

Ingredients

butter
4 eggs
water
salt and pepper to taste

Procedure

1. Butter 4 small heatproof custard cups or ramekins. Break the eggs into the cups.

2. Put about ½ inch of water into a medium skillet or pot. Bring to a low simmer. Carefully place the cups in the skillet and cover. Cook, just until the tops of the eggs are no longer liquidy (you want the yolks to still be runny inside), 3–5 minutes. Season with salt and pepper to taste.

3. Serve immediately with toast and little sausage cakes if you like.

Makes 2–4 servings.

title of "Mrs." Traditionally, the cook ruled her domain with an iron hand, cooking dishes from memory and often keeping them secret, even from the maids who assisted her. Indeed, as late as 1950, when the Queen Mother asked for a recipe from her palace cook, she was denied!

Cheese Muffins

Traditional English muffins are a lot like yeast-risen crumpets. This popular English cheddar recipe is quick to make and just as quick to satisfy, expecially when slathered with butter.

Breakfast Prayers

Breakfast often began with both servants and family praying together for a full 15 minutes. Everyone would kneel, resting their elbows on the dining-room chairs. Sometimes children tried to pick a chair near a window, so they could distract themselves during prayers.

Ingredients

2 cups flour, plus extra for dusting
1½ teaspoons baking powder
¼ teaspoon salt
⅛ teaspoon cayenne pepper
2 eggs
¾ cup milk
½ cup grated sharp cheddar

Procedure

1. Preheat oven to 400°F. Sift the 2 cups flour, baking powder, salt, and cayenne pepper together into a medium bowl.
2. Beat one egg lightly in a small bowl, then add the milk.
3. Add the milk mixture to the flour mixture and combine. Stir in the cheese.
4. Roll out onto a floured board and cut into rounds. Place the rounds on an ungreased baking sheet. Add the second egg to the empty liquid bowl and beat lightly. Brush the tops of the muffins with the egg.
5. Bake for 10–12 minutes. Serve still warm, split, and spread with butter. (These are also good with cheese.)

Makes 12 muffins.

The Shifting Breakfast Hour

As the nineteenth century progressed and the Industrial Revolution took hold, more people, especially those in the growing cities, began to work in factories. Because they had to spend time traveling to work each morning, breakfast became a lighter, more hurried, and earlier meal, moving from the traditional nine or ten A.M. to about seven or eight A.M.

Little Sausage Cakes

The English call sausages bangers *and frequently eat them for breakfast. Even in Mary's day sausages would have been available in links from the butcher in Thwaite Village nearby. Or perhaps Cook prepared these country cakes herself, by combining farm-raised meat and garden herbs, then sizzling them up into a savory morning treat. These sausage cakes are flavored with sage, a favorite herb with English cooks.*

Ingredients

½ pound ground pork (fatty pork is best)
2 small or medium sage leaves, chopped fine
¼ teaspoon salt
¼ teaspoon freshly ground pepper
⅛ teaspoon dried marjoram
⅛ teaspoon nutmeg
flour for dusting
vegetable oil for frying

What Do I Do with the Leftover Sage?

Fresh sage comes in bunches, and since you need only 2 leaves for this recipe, you will have leftover sage. Don't throw it out! You can dry it, just as cooks did in Mary's day. They would cut some of the sage from their kitchen herb garden before winter and dry it. This way they could season food during the colder months, when the herb could not grow. You can dry sage at home by bundling the stems

Procedure

1. Combine the pork, sage, salt, pepper, marjoram, and nutmeg in a medium bowl. Mix with your hands until well combined. Form into six small cakes or patties, not more than 1 inch thick.
2. Put some flour on a plate and lightly press both sides of each cake into the flour. Shake off any extra flour. The cakes should be only very lightly covered.
3. Heat a large, heavy skillet over high heat. Pour in just enough oil to coat the bottom of the pan. Carefully add the sausage cakes, one at a time, so that they do not touch. Fry until browned on both sides and just cooked through, about 3 minutes on each side. You will know they are done when there is no pink left in the center.
4. Serve warm with coddled eggs and toast.

Makes 6 sausage cakes.

Dried sage

together with a string, then hanging the bundle upside down to dry. Use the dry, crumbly leaves in place of fresh sage. Remember, though, that because all the moisture is gone, dried sage is at least twice as strong as fresh sage.

Cocoa

Before Cadbury's cocoa powder appeared in 1866, preparing hot cocoa was a time-consuming process. After the beans were ground into "nibs," they were pounded and stewed for hours in water. When the mixture had cooled, the white cocoa butter, which had separated from the chocolate, was removed. Then the chocolate was boiled again with milk and flavorings such as vanilla or cinnamon. Finally the mixture

Cocoa

Although tea was the national beverage of England, chocolate was also very popular. Children drank hot cocoa out of teacups at breakfast or right before going to bed.

This recipe is made the way a Victorian Cadbury's cocoa ad suggests, by whisking together cocoa powder, sugar, milk, and water. You may be used to one of the many brands of lump-free sweetened cocoa products on the market today. But the best-quality cocoa is still unsweetened, as it was in Colin's day, and is well worth the little whisking it needs to get rid of the lumps. Once you enjoy the taste of real cocoa powder, you'll be spoiled forever. And while cocoa products may have changed over the last century, we still need to abide by the nineteenth-century warning: If you burn the milk, you ruin the cocoa!

Ingredients

1 cup unsweetened cocoa powder
⅓–½ cup sugar, depending on how
    sweet you like it
3 cups milk
1 cup water

Procedure

1. Stir together the cocoa powder and sugar in the bottom of a ceramic pitcher or, if not available, in a small bowl.
2. Put the milk and water into a small pot. Bring to just below a boil (called scalding), stirring frequently. Turn off the heat.
3. Carefully add a ladleful of the hot liquid to the chocolate mixture. Whisk vigorously into a smooth, thin paste, to help prevent lumps. Pour the remaining hot liquid into the pitcher or, if you are using a bowl, add the chocolate mixture to the pot, whisking until smooth.
4. Pour hot cocoa into teacups and serve immediately. Add a sprinkle of cinnamon if you like.

Makes 4 teacups.

A cocoa plant; the cocoa beans are in the pod

was thickened with beaten eggs. Now you could drink it! Cadbury's premade cocoa powder changed all that. All you had to do now was add milk, water, and sugar, heat, and voilà!— *hot chocolate.*

"*I shall come back this afternoon,*" *Mary said, looking all round at her new kingdom, and speaking to the trees and the rose-bushes as if they heard her.*

Then she ran lightly across the grass, pushed open the slow old door and slipped through it under the ivy. She had such red cheeks and such bright eyes and ate such a dinner that Martha was delighted.

"Two pieces o' meat an' two helps of puddin'!" she said. "Eh! mother will be pleased when I tell her what th' skippin'-rope's done for thee."

—The Secret Garden
Chapter 9

A Manor Lunch

Yorkshire Pudding
Roasted Fowl with Bread Sauce
Potato Snow
Welsh Rabbit
Cabinet Pudding
Jam Roly Poly

A Manor Lunch

In Victorian times, the gentry might consume up to five meals a day: Breakfast, an informal luncheon, tea, an elaborate dinner, and a light supper before bed. However, many Victorians—especially servants, agricultural workers, and children—ate three meals a day: Breakfast, a main midday meal, and high tea or an evening supper. Mary and Colin, like most upper-class children, were served their main midday meal, called lunch or dinner, in the nursery. If Colin's mother had been alive, she might have joined them.

A nursery manor lunch included meat, which was considered healthy for children, seasonal vegetables, followed by milk, a pudding, or perhaps a simple luncheon cake. In contrast, poorer children like Dickon often had only bread or porridge for lunch, or on better days a bacon sandwich.

Adults generally ate a light lunch, and had their main meal, a formal dinner at night, in the dining room. On special occasions, when guests were invited, lunch would be a fancier occasion of several courses lasting up to three hours. But generally lunch was considered the most casual of Victorian meals, a time when the remains from the previous night's dinner would be set out. Lunch might include minced mutton or game pies prepared from uneaten game. Of course all left-overs would be well garnished and disguised as another dish by the cook. In a more formal time, when even middle-class people had live-in help, this comparatively relaxed meal gave the adults of the house a time to socialize without servants hovering through each course.

If young members of the household joined the adults for the midday meal, manners were more important than the menu. When children behaved badly, it was considered a grave reflection on the mother. Children were expected to attain a happy medium— to be forward enough to answer questions directed at them, but not to chatter too much, laugh too loudly, or even initiate conversation. The minute the meal was over, children returned to the nursery, while the adults enjoyed coffee.

A LADY'S LUNCH
———
Salmon Mayonnaise

Galantine of Chicken

Potato Salad

Asparagus

Bread, Biscuits, and Cheese

Molded Spiced Pears

Ices

A SUNDAY FAMILY LUNCH
———
Croquettes of Veal and Ham

Cold Roast Beef

Salad

New Potatoes

Beetroot Pickles

Bread, Butter, and Cheese

Cabinet Pudding

Poem to a Yorkshire Pudding

*Dusta know! Tha's
  famous*

*Tha's etten, all ower
  t' land.*

*Wi' rast beef—an' a
  drop o' gravy,*

*Eee—tha does taste
  grand.*

*Thou 'as a lot o'
  relations,*

*Of iver shape, an'
  form.*

*Like yon haggis—
  now, he's conceited,*

*Thinks, he's tekken
  t'world bi storm.*

*He's in a bag, teed up,
  wi' string,*

*Nobbut a savoury—
  wi' bits of meat.*

*Na thee—tha's leet,
  an' fluffy,*

*An' thou can be etten,
  fot'seet.*

Yorkshire Pudding

*This world-famous dish was invented in Yorkshire in the
eighteenth century as a way to use the savory drippings
that fell from a spit-roasted joint of meat. Traditionally, it is
served with a roast, and the recipe remains virtually
unchanged, although there are endless variations. Many
sprinkle a few drops of raspberry vinegar on top. It is often
served as a first course, eaten on its own with thick gravy.
However you decide to serve it, always cook Yorkshire
pudding right before you eat it, because it deflates quickly.*

Ingredients

2 large eggs
¾ cup milk
¼ cup water
1 cup flour
generous pinch of salt
about 2 tablespoons meat drippings or softened
    unsalted butter

Procedure

1. Preheat oven to 450°F.
2. In a medium bowl, whisk together the eggs, milk, and water. Whisk in the flour and salt, just until combined.
3. Spread an 11-by-7-inch baking pan with the meat drippings or butter and place in the oven for 5–7 minutes.
4. Very carefully, pour the batter into the pan and immediately close the oven. Cook until very puffed and nicely browned on the top, about 15 minutes. Remove from the oven. Carefully cut into squares and serve at once.

Serves 4–6.

Toad-in-the-Hole

Yorkshire pudding batter, mixed with leftover pieces of cooked meat or sausages and then baked, is a delicious meal called toad-in-the-hole. This traditional variation on Yorkshire pudding was often served at English boarding schools, and sodden versions of it have given it a bad reputation with English children. However, using little sausage cakes, toad-in-the-hole makes a tasty dish, slightly crisp on the outside, custardy inside.

Many Victorians took their chickens and large joints of meat to a butcher's shop for him to roast in his oven. But carefully tended fire-roasted meat was considered superior in flavor. For a kitchen with an open range, roasting required skill. As there was no thermostat to determine the strength of the heat, it took experience gauging the intensity of the fire and adjusting the meat the proper distance from the heat.

Roasted Fowl with Bread Sauce

When Mrs. Medlock, the housekeeper, brings a plump roasted fowl with creamy bread sauce to Colin's room, she can't understand why he and Mary turn it down. The dish was quite special, combining a flavorful spit-roasted chicken with a thick, rich bread sauce. Little did Mrs. Medlock know that Colin and Mary were eating extra food out in the garden!

Ingredients

Chicken
4½-pound roasting chicken, neck and giblets removed
4 tablespoons butter, softened
salt and pepper

Bread Sauce
4 tablespoons dried bread crumbs
2 tablespoons grated onion
¼–½ teaspoon salt, to taste
1½ cups half-and-half
1 tablespoon butter
generous pinch of cayenne pepper

Procedure

1. Preheat oven to 375°F. Rinse and pat dry the chicken. Rub all over with the butter, pushing some of it under the breast skin.
2. Generously salt and pepper the cavity and skin. Tie the legs together with a string and place, breast side up, on the rack of a roasting pan. Cover lightly with foil.
3. Roast for 1 hour, then remove the foil. Continue roasting for 20–30 minutes, or until the thickest part of the thigh exudes clear juices when pricked deeply with a fork. Baste occasionally.
4. Remove the chicken from the oven when done and let sit 10 minutes.
5. While the chicken is sitting, combine all the ingredients for the bread sauce in a small pot and boil for 2–3 minutes until thickened, stirring occasionally.
6. Carve the chicken and pass the bread sauce on the side.

Serves 6.

The Natural Chicken

One common complaint for Victorian cooks was of "battery" breeding, which was the raising of fowl in confined cages. This style of raising chickens became popular during the nineteenth century, although it led to tasteless chicken. Today we have the same complaints, compounded by the addition of the chemicals given to battery-bred birds. Free-range or organic chickens are the closest most c___ can get to the fu_____ the farm chicken that Colin and Mary would have eaten.

Potato Snow

Potatoes were a popular Victorian vegetable, often served at breakfast, lunch, and dinner. In fashionable homes, to break the monotony, it was essential to serve them a unique way each time; hence this lovely light pile of potatoes was invented.

A Meager Lunch

While potatoes were a small part of the varied diet served to the rich, for poorer Victorians potatoes, bread, and oatmeal were the primary foods. Sometimes cottagers' children ate porridge flavored with onion and vegetables, or simply a big plate of potatoes for lunch.

Ingredients

4 baking potatoes, peeled
salted water
4 tablespoons butter, softened
salt and freshly ground pepper, to taste
parsley

Procedure

1. Put the potatoes into a large pot and cover with lightly salted water. Bring to a boil and cook until the potatoes are quite soft, about 30 minutes.
2. Drain the potatoes and leave in a warm place to dry, or dry carefully with a kitchen towel.
3. Push the potatoes with a wooden spoon through a coarse sieve or ricer directly onto a serving plate, letting them pile high into a snowy mountain shape.
4. Serve immediately, but don't shake the plate, as the potatoes will settle. Top with butter, salt, and pepper, and garnish with parsley.

Makes 4–5 servings.

A Victorian vegetable dish

A Ladies' Lunch

Upper- and middle-class women didn't hold jobs, so they ate lunch at home. Luncheons became popular in the mid-nineteenth century, as an economical way to entertain. Lunch was less expensive to serve than dinner because food had to be comparatively light and easy to handle, as ladies ate without removing their jackets or bonnets. Easy-to-eat dishes, such as chicken salad, and gelatin molded with fresh fruit, were especially popular.

Rabbit or Rarebit?

This dish is often mistakenly called Welsh rarebit. The confusion may date back to a joke made in Mr. Francis Grose's 1785 Classical Dictionary of the Vulgar Tongue, in which it was defined as "bread and cheese toasted, i.e. a Welch rare bit," meaning a rare delicacy. Using a more expensive ingredient in a recipe's name was not uncommon, and shows up in America in a recipe called Cape Cod Turkey, which was actually made with fish!

Welsh Rabbit

Welsh rabbit, a toasted cheese dish, became quite popular in the nineteenth century, sometimes served as a "savoury," after dessert. Sometimes, though, Victorian children ate a "rabbit" for lunch or tea. Occasionally they dipped the toast into the tasty melted cheese mixture, which would have been served from a special dish set above hot water, to keep the cheese melted. You can enjoy it that way as well.

Ingredients

3 ounces coarsely grated cheddar, about 1 cup
1 tablespoon unsalted butter
1½ teaspoons milk
pinch of dry mustard
2 slices of bread

Procedure

1. Preheat the broiler.
2. Combine the cheddar, butter, milk, and mustard in a small saucepan. Melt over very low heat, stirring continuously with a wooden spoon until smooth, about 5 minutes.
3. Place the bread on a small ungreased baking sheet and toast under the broiler on one side very briefly, just until it starts to brown. Remove from the broiler and carefully turn the bread over. Divide the melted-cheese mixture over the bread. (Don't worry if it drips over the side; the browned bits that stick to the sheet are part of the fun.) Broil until the top is bubbly and beginning to brown, about 1 minute. Remove each rabbit to a plate with a spatula.
4. Serve immediately.

Makes 2 portions.

Leftovers

As the week progressed, leftover meat would reappear each day in various guises. This practice was so common, there is an old English saying that explains how a large Sunday joint would be served each day of the week:

Hot on Sunday,

Cold on Monday,

Hashed on Tuesday,

Minced on Wednesday,

Curried on Thursday,

Broth on Friday,

Cottage pie Saturday.

Pudding as a Staple

The English are enamored of puddings. Especially for the poor household, a filling yet inexpensive pudding was a vital part of the daily menu. Every day the frugal housewife would serve one of the infinite variations of rice or suet pudding. That way, when little other food was served, no one had to leave the table hungry.

Cabinet Pudding

In England, the word "pudding" can refer to any dessert. This showy period pudding, befitting the fanciest cabinet (government) feast, is a tasty example of a steamed English custard. Once unmolded, cabinet pudding is also splendid to behold, with its colorful layers of dried fruit and cookies.

No Victorian kitchen was complete without a variety of deep pudding molds, but they are uncommon in American kitchens today. Any small deep mold will do, but it is fun to assemble this pudding in a 2-cup glass measure or clear-plastic bowl, because you can look through and decoratively assemble ingredients as you work.

Ingredients

butter for greasing
20 glacé cherries, cut in half
8 strips of candied orange rind
18 soft ladyfingers
4 coconut macaroons
⅓ cup raisins
1 tablespoon sugar
1 teaspoon cornstarch
4 eggs
1 cup milk
¾ cup heavy cream
1 teaspoon vanilla extract
jam sauce (see p. 42)

Procedure

1. Butter a 2-cup glass measure or clear-plastic cup. Cut a small round of waxed paper to fit the bottom. Butter both sides, then place on the bottom of the cup.

2. Using some of the raisins, cherry halves, and the orange rind, make a decorative pattern on the bottom of the cup.

3. Gently press the ladyfingers on top of the fruit to form one layer, breaking them to fill in the gaps. Crumble 1 macaroon over the top, followed by a layer of decorative fruit. Repeat these layers until you are almost at the top, finishing off with a layer of ladyfingers. For an attractive pudding, make sure to add the dried fruit in layers against the glass.

4. Whisk together the sugar and cornstarch in a medium bowl to remove all the lumps. Whisk in the eggs, then the milk, cream, and vanilla.

5. Slowly pour the custard mixture over the layered cookies and fruit, stopping occasionally to allow the custard to seep into the nooks. Let settle for 15 minutes, then top off with the custard. Cover the top with buttered foil, using an elastic band or string to tie the foil to the cup.

6. In a pot large enough to hold the mold, bring 2 inches of water to a boil. Reduce to a simmer and carefully place the mold in the center. Tightly cover the pot and steam, in water that barely bubbles at the edges, for 1 hour.

7. When the cup is cool enough to handle, remove the foil and let sit for 15 minutes. Run a sharp knife around the edge of the mold. Place a plate over the top and invert the plate and mold. Carefully remove the cup. Serve warm, with jam sauce.

Makes 8 portions.

Christmas Pudding

Christmas pudding is the classic English holiday dessert. Traditionally, it was prepared on Advent Sunday, also called Stirrup Sunday, about a month before Christmas. During preparation, every member of the family in descending order of age stirred it in a clockwise direction. Each person made three wishes, one of which could be granted. The pudding was then boiled for hours in a linen cloth. On Christmas Day it was served with brandy or custard sauce.

Jam Roly Poly

A wide variety of steamed suet puddings, such as spotted dick (the "spots" are currants), were very popular in Victorian England. Jam roly poly, a log of jam-filled crust topped with a jam or custard sauce, was considered the quintessential nursery pudding.

Steamed suet puddings were actually wrapped in floured linen and boiled for a long time, giving them a distinctive texture. With the arrival of standard ovens and uniform temperatures, baked roly poly also become popular in England, and has a flaky crust more like the kind Americans are accustomed to.

Ingredients

Roly Poly
1½ cups flour
¾ cup shredded suet (about 2½ ounces) or 2½
    ounces butter, cut into small pieces
1½ teaspoons baking powder
⅛ teaspoon salt
½ cup water, plus extra for sealing
1–4 tablespoons milk
butter for greasing
⅔ cup your favorite jam

Jam Sauce
1 cup apricot or strawberry or your favorite jam
1 tablespoon fresh lemon juice

Procedure

1. Preheat the oven to 450°F.
2. Combine the flour, suet, baking powder, salt, and ½ cup water in a medium bowl. Mix with your hands until combined. Add the milk, continuing to mix with your hands just until it comes together easily into a dough.
3. Press out the dough directly onto a lightly greased baking sheet, to a rectangle about 10 by 4 or 5 inches. Spread the jam over the dough, leaving a large border all around. Roll one long side over and over until it overlaps with the other long side. (Don't worry if you have a little tear; just use a piece of dough to repair it.) Seal the seam and the ends well, using a little water if necessary.
4. Bake for 20 minutes. Reduce the heat to 400°F., and continue to bake until very brown and crisp, about 15 minutes.
5. While the roly poly is baking, make the jam sauce. Combine the jam and lemon juice in a small pot. Place on the stove until ready to heat.
6. Remove the baked roly poly from the oven. Heat the jam sauce until it is liquidy, stirring occasionally, 3–5 minutes. Slice roly poly and serve warm, topped with jam sauce.

Makes 6 servings.

*whisked away!
It is said that the
Queen was unaware
of this custom until a
brave guest asked a
servant to return his
plate. Fortunately, after
she discovered what
had been happening,
the Queen stopped
this tradition.*

43

"*Look at that robin! There he is! He's been foragin'
for his mate.*"

*Colin was almost too late but he just caught sight
of him, the flash of red-breasted bird with something
in his beak. He darted through the greenness and into
the close-grown corner and was out of sight. Colin
leaned back on his cushion again, laughing a little.*

"*He's taking her tea to her. Perhaps it's five o'clock.
I think I'd like some tea myself.*"

—The Secret Garden
Chapter 21

An English Tea

A Proper Pot of Tea

Cucumber Tea Sandwiches

Scones

Fruit Tea Loaf

Lemon Curd Tartlettes

Brandy Snap Baskets with Whipped Cream

An English Tea

By the time Mary, Colin, and Dickon were growing up, afternoon tea was a well-established custom—so much so that Colin imagines the robin bringing tea to his mate at five o'clock. Interestingly, the history of tea is very connected to England's role in colonizing India, where Mary was born.

In the early seventeenth century, Dutch traders brought tea to England, but although it was greatly appreciated, it was too expensive for the average family to afford. So the English tried planting Chinese tea in India, part of their vast Empire, but it didn't grow in the Indian climate.

In the 1820s an important discovery was made: An indigenous tea plant was sighted in Assam, India. Soon tea plantations in India brought down the price of tea radically. Now that middle- and upper-class households could afford it, tea became popular anytime, but serving it with a variety of sweets and sandwiches soon became a daily afternoon ritual. The cost continued to drop, so by the 1840s working-class families, like Dickon's, consumed vast quantities of tea as well.

Teatime in England quickly took on a variety of forms. The rich and landed gentry, like those at Misselthwaite Manor, often enjoyed their tea between

Who Invented Teatime?

The custom of afternoon tea is credited to Anna, the seventh Duchess of Bedford, in the eighteenth century. Apparently she complained of a "sinking feeling" in the afternoon and used tea, sweets, and conversation as a cure.

four and five o'clock, with light sandwiches and a variety of cakes and other confections. More elaborate "at homes," held at five o'clock, were an occasion for ladies to socialize. For the poor, tea was not just an extra but sometimes the only hot food they consumed for the day. "High tea" became an end-of-the-day buffet-style dinner for working families. For those who could afford it, it might include meat, vegetables, and a pudding, with tea served beforehand or along with the food. In Dickon's beloved Yorkshire, high tea is sometimes still a hearty meal, with ham and cheese and cakes and tarts all served together.

The importance of tea and teatime to all the English—from cottagers like Dickon to manor children like Mary and Colin—cannot be underestimated. Daily teatime was something to look forward to, even if it was as simple as tea and bread with butter and jam.

Most essential was to start with a properly made pot of tea, brewed with loose leaves rather than the tea bags most Americans use. Some period books even say guests preferred tea brewed by the mistress of the house, as it was often badly prepared by servants!

The Curative Powers of Tea

"A nurse because she sees how one or two cups of tea . . . restore her patient, thinks that three or four cups will do twice as much. This is not the case at all; it is, however, certain that there is nothing yet discovered which is a substitute for the English patient for his cup of tea; he can take it when he can take nothing else, and he often can't take anything else, if he has it not."

—Florence Nightingale

Invalid Children

Delicate children like Colin were told to eat a wide variety of curative foods, which often included meat. One popular cure called for a dose of home-brewed malt liquor along with an egg and a piece of meat! We know Colin was fed beef tea and possibly some other invalid dishes, such as mulled eggs or koumiss, a buttermilk-and-sugar drink. Beef tea was made from lean meat steeped in cold water, then simmered. To make 1 pint of tea, 1 pound of beef was used.

A Proper Pot of Tea

Mrs. Medlock, the housekeeper, was considered an "upper" servant. She was responsible for running the household as well as looking after the preserved foods, linen, and china, which she would have kept under lock and key. Just as the cook had scullery and kitchen maids who worked for her, Mrs. Medlock supervised several housemaids. For the most part she did not interfere with Cook's domain. But in order to help out, she and her staff probably prepared tea, coffee, soft drinks, and bottled fruit jam in what was called the "still" room. This is the way Mrs. Medlock would have prepared tea for Mary and Colin each afternoon, and it is still the best technique.

Ingredients

boiling water for heating the pot, plus
    1 cup per person
1 rounded teaspoon loose tea leaves per person,
    plus one for the pot

Procedure

1. To warm the pot, half fill the teapot with boiling water. Let it stand several minutes until the pot is very hot, then pour the water out.

2. Place loose tea leaves in the pot. Pour in the boiling water and let the tea steep in a warm place for 3–5 minutes.

3. Stir the tea and strain into cups. Let people help themselves to milk and sugar, or lemon.

A tea plant

Tea Lovers

Between 1840 and 1890 the average tea consumption in England rose from 1.6 pounds per person annually to 5.7 pounds (about 4 cups a day per person). The British still drink an average of about 6 cups of tea per person per day!

**Other Tea
Sandwiches**

*The variety of
fillings and shapes
for tea sandwiches is
limited only by your
imagination. Some
classic English fillings
include sliced ham or
well-chopped chicken
salad and watercress
sprigs; but you can use
your favorite foods,
like peanut butter and
jelly, sliced cheese, or
tuna salad. Or try a
jelly roll tea spiral:
Spread raspberry or
strawberry jam on
extra-thin white or
whole wheat bread
and roll. Wrap in
plastic and chill for
an hour. Slice into
3–5 spirals.*

Cucumber Tea Sandwiches

*Dainty sandwiches are a classic accompaniment to tea, and
cucumber is a favorite filling. But since cucumber sandwiches
can become sodden, the secret is to make them as close to
teatime as possible, and go lightly on the filling. If not, you
risk the kind of comment Oscar Wilde, the famous Victorian
writer, made when presented with a plate of cucumber
sandwiches: "My dear, I asked for a cucumber sandwich,
not a loaf with a field in the middle of it."*

Ingredients

2 tablespoons butter, at room temperature
8 slices of thin white bread
1 cucumber or 2 kirby cucumbers, peeled and sliced
   very thin
salt and freshly ground pepper to taste

Procedure

1. Butter the bread evenly on one side. Top four slices with a thin layer of cucumber slices. Season with salt and pepper to taste. Top each sandwich with a slice of bread, buttered side down.
2. Cut off the crusts, then cut each sandwich corner to corner, to form four triangles. Or you can cut into diagonal halves, if you prefer.
3. Serve within 1 hour.

Makes 16 small tea sandwiches.

A cucumber vine

Birthday Teas

Tea parties were often held to celebrate children's birthdays. At these parties there was generally an iced sponge cake with candles on it, and special tea sandwiches. At tea parties children would also play games. One such game was "blind feeds blind": Two blindfolded children stood opposite each other, each holding a plate of little tea cakes. Each tried to feed the other with a spoon, and whoever dropped the least number won.

Nursery Teas

Children of Mary and Colin's class enjoyed tea in the nursery promptly at four o'clock. Nursery teas often included unfrosted sponge cakes with jam, scones, and finger sandwiches. As children's main meal was lunch, tea was supposed to hold them over until supper before bedtime.

Scones

Scones make classic tea fare. Serve them warm, right out of the oven, with jam and clotted cream. They can also be made beforehand, frozen raw, then cooked right out of the freezer: Just bake them a few extra minutes. For a variation, add ½ cup currants to make Yorkshire scones called "fat rascals." Clotted cream can be found in most specialty shops.

Ingredients

Scones
2 cups flour, plus extra for dusting
2 tablespoons sugar
2½ teaspoons baking powder
1 teaspoon salt
3 tablespoons cold unsweetened butter,
    cut into small pieces
⅔ cup milk

Glaze
milk
2 tablespoons sugar

Procedure

1. Preheat the oven to 450°F.
2. Whisk the flour, sugar, baking powder, and salt together in a large bowl. Mix in the butter with your hands, just until the dough resembles coarse bread crumbs. Add the milk and mix with your hands, until the dough is just moistened. Place the dough on a lightly floured work surface. Knead just until it comes together, about three or four times. Form into a ball.
3. Pat the dough out into a circle that is about ½ to ¾ inch thick. Cut into 12 wedges or rounds. With a spatula place the pieces on an ungreased baking sheet. Brush the tops with milk and sprinkle with sugar.
4. Bake until lightly browned, 8–12 minutes. Serve immediately.
5. Guests split the scones open and enjoy them with jam and clotted cream.

Makes 12 small wedge-shaped or round scones. As a variation for a dolls' tea party, cut the dough with a large thimble to make about 80 thimble scones. Bake for 5–7 minutes.

Baking Powder

In the mid-1850s, a quick-rising baking powder was developed in America. Until then, breads and cakes had been leavened with yeast, which required kneading and lots of time for the dough to rise. Because baking powder was so convenient, it became popular immediately. You could simply add a spoonful of the powder to the batter and bake—and voilà! *light tea cakes and breads in less than half the time. Baking-powder-risen cakes and buns soon became the ideal accompaniment to tea.*

Slow Walking Bread

Mary would have known tea loaf by its Yorkshire name, "slow walking bread." Perhaps it was given this name because it kept well during a long trip, in the days before quick transport, when even the nearest town was a good long walk away. Cake dense with dried fruit was also called "cut and come again cake," as it kept over a long period.

Fruit Tea Loaf

Tea in a cake? Yes! Cakes packed with dry fruit date back to well before The Secret Garden. *As tea became a kitchen staple always on hand, it was a handy ingredient to include too.*

Although this loaf is very easy to prepare, it needs to be started a day before baking.

Ingredients

1 cup water
1 rounded teaspoon black tea leaves or 1 tea bag
11 ounces mixed dried fruit
¼ cup raisins
⅔ cup dark brown sugar
¼ cup butter (½ stick) at room temperature, plus extra for greasing
2 cups flour, plus extra for dusting
1 egg
½ teaspoon baking soda
1 teaspoon baking powder

Procedure

1. Bring the water to a boil. Add the tea or tea bag and let it steep for 10 minutes. Strain the leaves or remove the tea bag and pour the tea into a large bowl.
2. If there are pits in the fruit, remove them by hand. Put all the fruit except the raisins into the food processor and pulse several times, just until chopped. (This can be done by hand as well.) Add the chopped fruit, raisins, and ⅓ cup brown sugar to the tea, stirring to combine. Cover and let sit at room temperature overnight.
3. Preheat the oven to 325°F. Butter a loaf pan. Line with waxed paper and butter again. Add a little flour to the pan and shake it around to cover lightly, then shake out any excess.
4. With a wooden spoon, mix the remaining ⅓ cup brown sugar and the ½ stick butter in a large bowl until creamy. Stir in the egg. Sift the 2 cups flour, baking soda, and baking powder into the bowl and mix, just until combined. Stir in all the fruit mixture, undrained.
5. Pour the batter into the prepared loaf pan and bake for an hour. Turn the heat down to 300°F. and continue baking until a knife inserted into the loaf comes out with just a few crumbs sticking to it, about 45–60 minutes. (If the top gets very dark during cooking, cover loosely with foil.) When cool enough to handle, invert the loaf pan and remove the waxed paper. Serve warm or at room temperature, with plenty of butter.

Makes 1 loaf.

Happy Homes

In happy homes where tea is brewed at five o'clock, or where indeed, it is always on tap, life is a success.

—Manners and Social Usage, *Mrs. John Sherwood, 1884*

Lemon Curd Tartlettes

*Little cakes and tarts were quite popular for afternoon tea,
and these are ideal—delicate, pretty, and very lemony.
Lemon curd is a spreadable filling and it's delicious on toast,
too. This recipe is especially easy to prepare, because the
dough is pressed into little muffin tins instead of being rolled
out.*

Ingredients

Lemon Filling
1 large egg
1 large egg yolk
¼ cup sugar
zest of 1 lemon
3 tablespoons fresh lemon juice
¼ cup butter (½ stick), chilled and cut into 4 pieces

Tart Dough
1 stick butter, softened, plus extra for greasing
⅓ cup confectioners' sugar
1 cup flour

Garnishes
small blueberries, raspberries, or slices of strawberry
mint leaves (optional)
candied violets or orange strips (optional)
small edible flowers (optional)

Procedure

1. Whisk together the egg, egg yolk, sugar, lemon zest, and juice in a small saucepan. Add the butter pieces and place over low heat. Cook about 10 minutes, stirring constantly with a rubber spatula to prevent sticking, until the mixture just coats the back of a spoon. Do not boil! Immediately remove from the heat and scrape into a small bowl. Press plastic wrap over the curd to prevent a skin from forming. Place in the refrigerator.

2. Preheat the oven to 350°F. Butter two shallow mini-muffin tins. Sift the confectioners' sugar and flour together into a medium bowl. Mix in the stick of butter with your fingers until it looks like fine bread crumbs. Place 1 tablespoon of the dough in each muffin cup. (Don't worry if it looks crumbly; it will come together.) Press the dough in each cup around the bottom and sides. Bake until lightly browned, 12–15 minutes. While the crust is still warm, indent the center of each tart with your thumb. Remove the tarts from the tins.

3. Fill the center of each tart with a heaping teaspoon of curd, leaving a border of dough around the edge. Top the center of each tart with one garnish—a berry or berry slice, a mint leaf, a candied violet, or a small edible flower, if you are using any of them.

Makes 24 tartlettes.

A lemon plant

Toy China Tea Sets

Just like American children, Mary may have played with miniature tea sets as a small child. These sets were originally created in the late 1800s by china manufacturers as sample sets for their salesmen. When the salesmen showed these pretty little sets to their customers, mothers bought them for their children.

Brandy Snap Baskets with Whipped Cream

Brandy snap batter is magical: You drop a gooey batter onto a baking sheet, and in about 5 minutes it comes out in thin lacy cookies that are moldable. You can roll warm brandy snaps around a wooden spoon before filling them with whipped cream in the traditional manner. Or, as here, in a pretty presentation, lacy brandy snap rounds can be formed into little baskets for an attractive teatime treat. Brandy snaps are often made with brandy; this recipe does not call for this ingredient, though.

Ingredients

Brandy Snap Batter
3 tablespoons sweet butter, plus extra for greasing
¼ cup dark brown sugar
1½ tablespoons light corn syrup
¼ cup plus 1 tablespoon flour
1¼ teaspoons ground ginger

Filling
¾ cup whipping cream
½ teaspoon vanilla extract
2 teaspoons sugar

Procedure

1. Preheat the oven to 350°F.
2. Grease a baking sheet lightly with butter. Have a mini-muffin tin ready beside the oven for molding the baskets while the snaps are still warm.
3. Combine the brown sugar, 3 tablespoons butter, and corn syrup in a small saucepan. Heat over low heat, stirring frequently, until melted and well combined. Stir in flour and ginger, just until combined.
4. Drop 4 level teaspoons of batter, one at a time, at least 3 inches apart, onto the greased baking sheet. Bake until lacy and very slightly darker on the edges, 5–7 minutes.
5. Remove the pan from the oven. As soon as you can, lift the brandy snaps with a metal spatula, then quickly place them, one at a time, in the muffin cups. Immediately, press gently down into the centers to form baskets. (If they get too hard to shape, don't panic; just place them back in the oven for a minute or two to soften.) Repeat with the remaining batter to complete the twelve baskets. Once cool, remove from muffin tins. These hold well, in a sealed container, for several hours before serving.
6. Just before serving, whip the cream, vanilla, and sugar in a clean bowl with a whisk or with an electric beater until soft peaks form.
7. Fill each basket with about a tablespoon of the whipped cream and garnish with broken cookie pieces. Serve immediately.

Makes 12 brandy snap baskets.

Ginger

**The Land of
Green Ginger**

*The Yorkshire port city
of Hull received huge
cargoes of spices from
foreign lands.
In fact, a street in
the old district of
Hull, where the rich
merchants lived,
is called the Land of
Green Ginger.*

At the end of the path Mary was following, there seemed to be a long wall, with ivy growing over it. She was not familiar enough with England to know that she was coming upon the kitchen-gardens where the vegetables and fruit were growing. She went toward the wall and found that there was a green door in the ivy, and that it stood open. This was not the closed garden, evidently, and she could go into it.

She went through the door and found that it was a garden with walls all round it and that it was only one of several walled gardens which seemed to open into one another. She saw another open green door, revealing bushes and pathways between beds containing winter vegetables. Fruit-trees were trained flat against the wall, and over some of the beds there were glass frames.

—The Secret Garden
Chapter 4

The Kitchen Garden

Fresh Spring Peas with Mint

Glazed Carrots

Summer Pudding

Two Fools

Raspberry Jam

Raspberry Vinegar

Molded Spiced Pears

Strawberries and Cream

The Kitchen Garden

By the turn of the century, when Mary was exploring her secret garden, the English kitchen garden had developed a staggering variety of plants. One turn-of-the-century seed catalogue lists 170 kinds of peas, 150 types of melon, and 58 kinds of beets!

Mary had to walk through Misselthwaite Manor's kitchen gardens before she discovered the secret garden. They were a good distance from the house, to hide the homely sight of vegetables and laboring gardeners from the view of the manor, and to contain the smell of the composting manure. Nevertheless, the kitchen gardens would have been a pleasant place for a stroll, with clean dry paths, shady areas for seating, flowers for color, fragrant herbs, and perhaps a few ornamental touches like a sundial or fountains.

A typical Victorian kitchen garden of an upper-class manor could be 1½–5 acres, depending on the size of the family, or as many as 25 acres for royal palaces. It required about six servants to maintain a 3-acre garden. This might seem immense, but in fact most Victorian families were quite large, and the garden had to be substantial enough to feed the whole household, which might easily consist of the parents, seven to ten children, a nanny, several nursery maids, a governess, and a tutor,

From the Garden

"Shopping" at Misselthwaite might have gone something like this: Cook would tell the journeyman, an underservant, what produce she needed for the day. The journeyman then went to the head gardener. Together they would gather vegetables and fruit; then the journeyman would carry them into the kitchen in two deep baskets hung from a yoke across his shoulders. He would unload them into

as well as twelve or more servants.

Half a typical kitchen garden, like Misselthwaite's, would be divided into four large flat areas, called quarters. Each quarter contained a different type of plant. The first might consist of herbs such as parsley, thyme, fennel, hyssop, comfrey, and southernwood. The second quarter might be root vegetables, such as horseradish, carrots, and parsnips. The third quarter might be given over to a variety of salad plants and greens, and also salad flavorings, such as garlic and shallots. The fourth quarter might hold plants that needed larger plots—asparagus and broccoli, for example. Field peas, beans, and cabbages might be grown outside the garden because they also needed more room. By contrast, simple kitchen gardens like Dickon's, surrounded by stones, were most likely placed conveniently near the house, where the cottager could chase away pests, or wherever there was space and the soil was best.

The unwalled half of the manor kitchen garden was typically made up of what was called the "slip garden." The slip garden was the space directly outside the walled garden. There was often a place to compost the ash, leaves, and garden rubbish into a rich compost for the garden. The slip garden was often used for hardy fruits and vegetables that needed space, like cherries, plums, rhubarb, and gooseberries.

slots in the vegetable storeroom. (Remember, no refrigerator!) Choice vegetables, such as little French beans or asparagus, would be placed in a shallow bowl with a little water, to keep them fresh.

The Pea Man

*Hot peas were
commonly sold from
carts in the streets
of nineteenth-century
England. The peas, in
their shells, were ladled
into bowls provided
by the pea man.
Customers dipped the
pods into melted
butter, then drew them
between their teeth
to extract the peas.*

Fresh Spring Peas with Mint

*The cool English climate is perfect for growing sweet, tasty
peas. The popular pea plant was dubbed "prince of the
vegetable garden," and was so well loved that many
Victorian recipes call for enormous quantities per person,
as many as 4 cups to serve two hearty eaters!*

*Fresh spring peas, sweetened with a touch of sugar and
perfumed with fresh mint, are an English favorite. They are
as tasty today as when Ben Weatherstaff harvested them
out of the kitchen garden a hundred years ago.*

Ingredients

½ cup water
4 sprigs of fresh mint
1 teaspoon sugar
1¼–1½ pounds whole peas, shelled (about 2 cups)
    or 1 package (10-ounces) frozen baby peas
1–2 teaspoons butter, to taste
salt and pepper to taste

Procedure

1. Combine the water, mint, and sugar in a small pot. Bring to a boil.
2. Add the peas and cover. When the water comes to a boil again, pull out a pea with a slotted spoon, blow on it, and taste. The pea should be tender and hot all the way through. If it is not, boil for another minute and try again. Drain the peas in a colander and discard the mint.
3. Pour the peas into a bowl and toss with the butter, salt, and pepper.
4. Eat immediately.

Serves 6–8.

A sprig of mint

Victorian Vegetables

Victorians ate an extraordinary variety of vegetables. We enjoy many of the same ones today, like asparagus, peas, carrots, beans, and potatoes. However, some were considerably more unusual and included cardoon, which looks like a giant celery; black-rooted scorzonera; and colewort, a small variety of cabbage.

Glazed Carrots

Besides being in simple side dishes, like the glazed carrots here, carrots were used in numerous ways, such as to add color to freshly churned butter.

Ingredients

3 carrots, peeled and sliced into rounds
1 cup chicken broth or 1 cup water and a generous
  pinch of salt
1 tablespoon butter
1 tablespoon (dark or light) brown sugar
salt and pepper to taste
ground nutmeg (optional)

Bad Produce

Today we take bad produce back to the market, or simply throw it out. But kitchen-garden life with servants had a complex pecking order. Colin finds the carrots woody and tasteless. First he complains to Mrs. Medlock, who talks to Cook, who airs her problem with the head gardener, who talks to the man in charge of vegetables in the greenhouse, who yells at the journeyman who delivered the vegetables!

Procedure

1. Place the carrots, broth, butter, and brown sugar in a heavy-bottomed pan.
2. Bring to a boil, then reduce heat to a rapid simmer, cooking over medium-high heat until almost all the liquid is evaporated, about 10–15 minutes. Continue cooking, carefully stirring or shaking the pan frequently, until the carrots start to brown a little, about an additional 5 minutes. Do not cook too long or they will burn.
3. Season to taste with salt and pepper, as well as with nutmeg if you like.
4. Serve hot as a side dish.

Serves 2–4.

Queen Anne's lace

Wild Carrots

Wild carrots are plentiful in both England and America. In England wild carrots are known as cow parsley or bird's-nest; here they are commonly called Queen Anne's lace, because of their light, frilly flower, which looks like crocheted lace. If you recognize this white lacy flower, pull up the entire plant and sniff the root; it smells like carrots!

Seasonal Eating

Although Misselthwaite probably had greenhouses to grow exotic fruit and to force produce early, most Victorians, like Dickon's family, ate berries and other produce only in season.

Before standard refrigeration and easy transport, a main concern of most rural people was to keep whatever they had grown from the end of one growing season to the first harvest. Fruit that would not keep, like berries, was often made into preserves. Cherries, gooseberries,

Summer Pudding

Although we tend to think of our concern for healthy eating as a recent development, people have made the connection between food and health for centuries. In the 1700s this pudding was invented as a kind of "health food" alternative to the typical and very rich suet pudding. It remained popular, particularly as an ideal use for the summer's berry crop.

Summer pudding is made in a bread-lined bowl filled with syrupy berries that are weighed down and left to soak overnight. The next day the pudding is inverted. It is gorgeous to look at, because the juicy fruit saturates the bread, turning it a bright-red color!

Colin and Mary may well have picked their own berries from the manor's large kitchen garden and then enjoyed this pudding for dessert with their lunch.

Ingredients

1½ pints fresh raspberries or fresh mixed raspberries and blueberries
½ cup sugar
butter for greasing
10–12 slices firm-textured white bread, crusts removed

Procedure

1. Combine the raspberries and sugar in a small pot. Heat over medium heat, stirring occasionally, but very gently, 3 or 4 times, just until the sugar is melted, about 3 minutes. Remove from the heat. (If you are using blueberries as well, slightly mash them first with the sugar over medium heat. When the sugar is melted, add the raspberries and stir gently, just until the raspberries are shiny, 1–2 minutes.)

2. Butter a 3-cup bowl. Line the bowl with the bread, overlapping the slices generously, so that none of the bowl shows through at all. Cut the bread in halves to fit in the bowl, if necessary. Reserve the remaining bread for the top.

3. When the berries have cooled, pour off about 3 tablespoons of the syrup into a small bowl, cover, and chill. Pour the rest of the berries and juice into the bowl. Top with the remaining bread, overlapping it generously so that you don't see any of the berries below. Crimp the sides of the bread in to conform with the shape of the bowl.

4. Place a plate, slightly smaller than the diameter of the bowl, directly on the top bread slices. Weigh this down with two cans or whatever heavy items you have on hand. Refrigerate overnight.

5. Place a plate on the top of the bowl, then invert the bowl with the plate. Remove the bowl. If there are any slices that are not soaked through, drench them with the reserved berry juice. Cut the pudding into wedges and serve cold with whipped cream if you like.

Serves 6–8.

Raspberries

and currants were dried.
Root vegetables like carrots, potatoes, and turnips were often kept in a root cellar, which would ideally be cool and moderately dry in any season. To make these nourishing vegetables last, they were often completely buried in sand. Leafy vegetables, like cabbage, were partly covered in sand.

Garden Cures

Most kitchen gardens had a plot devoted to medicinal plants and herbs. These would be steeped in hot water or combined into pastes or dried and ground into powders, and used to treat various injuries and illnesses.

Here are just a few of the many Victorian herbal cures: balm for headaches and bee stings; betony for aches and pains; chamomile for indigestion; comfrey for a poultice under a bandage for sprains and swellings; goldenrod to bathe cuts and scratches; mallow to bathe sores or to

Two Fools

Fools are made with tangy fruit, often gooseberries, and whipped cream. They are simple desserts, easy to concoct, using your favorite sweetened cooked fruit. The recipes below can easily be doubled.

Ingredients

For Cranberry Fool:
½ cup fresh or frozen cranberries
2–3 tablespoons sugar, depending on how tart you like it
1 teaspoon butter
½ cup heavy cream

For Apricot Fool:
¼ cup apricot jam
⅓ cup heavy cream

Procedure

To make the Cranberry Fool:

1. Put the cranberries, sugar, and butter into a small pot. Cook over medium heat, stirring occasionally, until the cranberries burst and soften, about 3–5 minutes (if frozen, about 5–10 minutes). Take off the heat and stir.
2. When the cranberries are just slightly warm or at room temperature, whip the cream until it forms stiff peaks. This can be done by hand or with a mixer. Don't overbeat, or the cream will separate and turn into butter and buttermilk!
3. With a rubber spatula, gently mix the cranberries into the cream, just until combined. Serve immediately in small dessert bowls.

To make the Apricot Fool:

1. Place the jam in a microwave-proof bowl. Heat on high, uncovered, until just melted, about 1 minute. Stir.
2. Follow steps #2 and #3 above.

Makes 2 servings.

drink for bladder problems; rosemary to soothe the nerves and for headaches and insomnia; tansy for a wide variety of illnesses, including indigestion; and wormwood as a general tonic and blood cleanser.

Garden Thieves

The typical kitchen garden had high walls, to provide excellent support for fruit trees and also valuable protection against both animals and thieves. Sometimes, to prevent stealing, drastic measures were used. The tops of the walls were smeared with an indelible mixture of red ocher and grease. In the days when children often had only one pair of pants, the next step was to keep your eyes peeled for passing trouser seats!

Raspberry Jam

Raspberry jam was a part of Colin's manor house breakfast: "He wakened each morning with an amazing appetite and the table near his sofa was set with a breakfast of home-made bread and fresh butter, snow-white eggs, raspberry jam and clotted cream."

Big vats of jam were cooked after the berry harvest, then preserved in sealed jars to enjoy through the winter when fresh fruit wasn't as common. This recipe is easily doubled.

Ingredients

½ cup sugar
½ pint raspberries

Procedure

1. Preheat the oven to 250°F.
2. Put the sugar into an ovenproof bowl and place it in the oven for 5–7 minutes.
3. While the sugar is warming, put the raspberries into a small saucepan. Over medium heat, cook until the juices come to a boil, about 2–5 minutes.
4. Carefully add the warm sugar to the raspberries and bring to a boil. Continue boiling for 5 minutes. Pour into a small bowl or jar. When the jam is at room temperature, chill it. Store the jam in the refrigerator for up to a week.

Makes about ½ cup.

Dickon's Cottage Garden

"The secret garden was not the only one Dickon worked in. Round the cottage on the moor there was a piece of ground enclosed by a low wall of rough stones. Early in the morning and late in the fading twilight and on all the days Colin and Mary did not see him, Dickon worked there planting or tending potatoes and cabbages, turnips and carrots and herbs for his mother."

—The Secret Garden
Chapter 24

Raspberry Vinegar

Yorkshire people often serve a few drops of this sweet and fruity vinegar over their Yorkshire pudding. This vinegar is more like a syrup than what we call a vinegar; to make a raspberry vinegar that can be used in salad dressing, reduce the amount of sugar to 2–4 tablespoons.

Ingredients

½ pint fresh raspberries
about ¾ cup white wine vinegar or distilled vinegar
½ cup sugar

Mr. Weatherstaff's Fruit Picker

By the beginning of the nineteenth century, gardening manuals started to advertise tools to help pick hard fruit like apples and pears. One such tool was a combination tweezers and scissors that sat on a pole and was activated by levers and pulleys, so you could cut the branch and then hold on to it. That way the only person touching the fruit would be the person eating it, or Cook.

74

Procedure

1. Place the berries in a 2-cup glass measure or in a small glass, ceramic, or stainless steel bowl. Cover with the vinegar, then seal with plastic wrap. Leave at room temperature for two to three days, stirring gently once or twice a day.
2. Place three layers of cheesecloth in a strainer. Strain the vinegar into a small pot. Do not press down on the berries, or the vinegar will become cloudy. Discard the berries.
3. Add the sugar, turn the heat to high, and bring to a boil, stirring frequently until the sugar is dissolved, about 2–3 minutes. Strain again through cheesecloth or a very fine sieve. Using a funnel, pour into a small pretty bottle. This ruby-colored vinegar will keep indefinitely.

Makes about ¾ cup.

The Vinegar Cure

Raspberry vinegar was a popular Victorian cure for congested lungs and sore throats. A large spoonful or two would be mixed in a glass of water and drunk to ease a cough or congested chest, and to cool a fever. It was also considered an excellent gargle for sore throats.

Ice, Anyone?

Molded Spiced Pears

This adaptation of a recipe from the popular Mrs. Beeton's Book of Household Management *is an easy and fun way to use the kitchen-garden pear harvest. The dessert features a flower of poached pear halves suspended in spiced pear-apple gelatin. The recipe requires 8 hours to gel properly before eating, but is well worth the wait.*

Mary and Colin might have enjoyed this for lunch in Colin's room; it also makes a light alternative to traditional Christmas-dinner desserts.

Ingredients

1 quart apple juice
¼ cup raspberry jam
1 cinnamon stick or pinch of ground cinnamon
4 whole cloves or pinch of ground cloves
3 small Bosc pears
1 package (2½ teaspoons) plus 1 teaspoon
    unflavored gelatin
¼ cup cold water

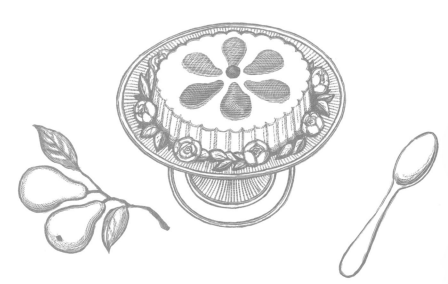

76

Procedure

1. Put the apple juice, raspberry jam, cinnamon, and cloves into a small pot. Bring to a simmer and whisk to combine.
2. While this poaching liquid is heating, peel the pears. Halve them lengthwise and remove their cores with a spoon. As each is prepared, drop it into the poaching liquid to prevent browning.
3. Bring the poaching liquid to a boil. Immediately reduce to a simmer and partly cover. Cook until the pears are soft and fork tender but not falling apart, about 30–45 minutes.
4. Remove the pears from the liquid with a slotted spoon. Pour the liquid through a sieve lined with cheesecloth or a coffee filter. Return 2½ cups of the strained liquid to the rinsed pot. Place the gelatin in a small bowl and whisk together with the cold water. Let sit for 5 minutes, until it is spongy. Heat the poaching liquid and add a few tablespoons to the gelatin, whisking until very well combined.
5. Pour all the gelatin into the hot poaching liquid.
6. Wet an 8-inch cake pan. Drain out the water, but leave the pan moist. Arrange the pears in a circle, rounded sides down and wide ends facing out to the edges. Carefully pour the liquid into the mold. Cover with plastic wrap and let set in the refrigerator overnight.
7. Fill a sink or a large bowl with hot water. Carefully place the mold in the water for a few seconds. Place a plate, preferably glass, on top of the mold and invert onto the plate. Remove the mold. Serve immediately or refrigerate uncovered until ready to serve.

Serves 4–6.

until the fall. Easiest of all, ice could be purchased from the local fishmonger, who had to keep blocks of it on hand to keep his fish fresh.

Indoors, ice could be kept cold in an ice chest. Ice was placed in a small, shelved chest, along with perishables. As the ice melted, the water would drain out through a channel built into the bottom of the box. Some form of icebox was used here and in England until as late as the 1950s!

The Greenhouse

The desire for exotic fruit led to the eighteenth-century development of the greenhouse. Greenhouses supplied the wealthy with tropical and out-of-season produce, something we take for granted today. A well-organized kitchen garden could provide salads for Christmas, asparagus in the fall, and luxuries like grapes, melons, figs, and peaches all year round.

Strawberries and Cream

Freshly picked berries, juicy and still warm from the sun, are still best savored as they were in Victorian times, tossed in sugar and topped with cream. Pick your own, or look for locally raised ripe strawberries that are deep red and small. If you can, top them with clotted cream, a favorite of Colin's. This thick, rich cream can be found in most specialty shops.

Ingredients

1 pint fresh ripe strawberries
sugar to taste
heavy or clotted cream

Procedure

1. Wash the strawberries. Remove the top green (the hulls) with your thumbnail and index finger or a knife. Cut the strawberries in half lengthwise.
2. Place the strawberries in a bowl and toss with sugar. The amount of sugar will depend on the tartness of the berries. Let sit for 10 minutes, then pour the cream on top.
3. Eat immediately.

Makes 2–4 servings.

Tea with the Queen

Queen Victoria's state-of-the-art kitchen garden was huge—31 acres that needed 150 gardeners to maintain it! It had 12-foot outer fruit walls, a 1,000-foot terrace, and a 30-foot fountain in the center. The Queen often drove the 1½ miles from her castle to the garden in her pony carriage. She would stop for tea at the head gardener's cottage, in a special room set aside for the royal family's visits. There she might take a simple tea of strawberries and cream, along with a cup of tea, of course.

"*I'll tell thee what, lad,*" *Mrs. Sowerby said when she could speak.* "*I've thought of a way to help 'em. When tha' goes to 'em in th' mornin tha' shall take a pail o' good new milk an' I'll bake 'em a crusty cottage loaf or some buns wi' currants in 'em, same as you children like. Nothin's so good as fresh milk an' bread. Then they could take off th' edge o' their hunger while they were in their garden an' th' fine food they get indoors 'ud polish off th' corners.*"

"*Eh! mother!*" *said Dickon admiringly,* "*what a wonder tha' art! Tha' always sees a way out o' things. They was quite in a pother yesterday. They didn't see how they was to manage without orderin' up more food—they felt that empty inside.*"

—The Secret Garden
Chapter 24

Dickon's Cottage Food

Tattie Broth

Pease Pudding

Yorkshire Oatcakes

Cottage Loaf

Dough-Cakes with Brown Sugar

Parkin

Dickon's Cottage Food

All through *The Secret Garden*, Dickon's cottage life is sharply contrasted to the world of Misselthwaite Manor. Yorkshire cottagers, like Dickon's family, generally lived on porridge, oatcakes, bread, and whatever they could raise. Meat as a main course was not common, although some cottagers owned pigs and chickens, which added variety to their diet. Milk—for drinking, butter, or cheese—was available only if a family owned a milking animal or had the wages to purchase milk.

Cottages like Dickon's date back a thousand years. Traditionally they were the homes of people who were servants to the lord of the manor, like Mr. Craven. Dickon's four-room cottage may seem small for fourteen, but many families lived in one room only. All the cooking, washing, and sewing had to be done in that room. But whatever the size of the house, cottage kitchen hearths, which provided food and warmth, became the heart of the family.

Dickon's mother used the kitchen hearth, which was much like a fireplace and may have been enclosed with metal grates, to cook seasonal foods. In the summer she prepared fresh fruits and vegetables that didn't store well over the winter. (In this way her family was far more fortunate than many in London, who couldn't get

Cottage Magic and Myths

Magic is part of The Secret Garden *and well known to country cottagers of the moor. Like other cottagers, Dickon might have known garden spells or charms to make cream turn to butter in the churn. He may also have believed in the "bar-quest," a doglike animal with lamplike eyes, that could be a protecting or evil spirit, or in serpents called "worms," and dragons whose poisonous breath could kill.*

their hands on fresh produce at all!) What wasn't eaten immediately was preserved. Berries were made into fruit jams and garden herbs into homemade medicines. Wild foods such as bilberries, honey, and grouse, which were fresh and free, were also gathered whenever possible.

When the warm growing season was over, foods that kept well, like cabbages, carrots, turnips, and potatoes, were stored over the winter. During the cold months the iron pot that hung over the hearth bubbled with whatever was on hand: tattie broth, pease porridge, or winter vegetable stew. The hungriest months were in the late winter, when the stored food ran low and the growing season had not begun. During this time Cook might have sold Susan Sowerby "drippings," the fat that dripped off the large joints of meat at Misselthwaite, to either cook or resell to purchase family necessities that couldn't be grown.

On the one hand, the cottage diet was extremely limited. But on the other, everything was freshly made from scratch. So once a week, on their baking day, Dickon and his siblings enjoyed warm cottage loaves, fresh from the oven; little buns loaded with sweet currants; or parkin, a Yorkshire gingerbread that grew even tastier and stickier each day it sat.

Manor Cottage Parties

Owners of some large manors, like Mr. Craven of Misselthwaite, often celebrated a grand occasion—a wedding, for example—with their cottagers. One such party was held for 300. The estate provided tenants with beef, plum pudding, and ale, followed by a dance, supper, and fireworks.

Soup for the Poor

*During the last years
of the Victorian era
imports of cheap
meat and corn drove
the English farming
industry into a
depression. To help
the poor, large
country houses like
Misselthwaite Manor
provided aid. Soup
made in the manor
was taken to the church
in a pony cart and
distributed after church
services. And in many
parishes farmworkers'
children went once a
week to the local
manor, where they were
given scraps of food
and meat drippings for
their mothers.*

Tattie Broth

*Compared with Misselthwaite's kitchen garden, Dickon's
small plot of land, surrounded by rough stones, produced little
variety. But because he was a natural gardener, his plot was
productive enough so that that even in the winter months,
there were plenty of "tatties" to provide healthy and filling
fare for his large family.*

*Like other cottagers, Dickon's family probably didn't eat
meat except on special occasions. Instead, a little bacon or,
if a family kept a cow, a touch of fresh butter might be used
to flavor stews, puddings, and filling soups like this one.
Dickon's mother might have added whatever else was on
hand to this cottager's soup, such as cabbage and turnips.
Feel free to do the same, adding extra water if necessary.*

Ingredients

2 tablespoons butter or 3 slices of chopped uncooked
  bacon
1 onion, sliced
2 large potatoes, peeled and diced
3 cups water or chicken broth
1 teaspoon salt
carrot, grated
2 teaspoons chopped parsley leaves (optional)
salt and pepper to taste

Procedure

1. Melt the butter or cook the bacon in a small pot over a medium heat. Add the onion and cook, stirring occasionally, until it starts to brown, 5–10 minutes.
2. Add the potatoes, water or broth, and 1 teaspoon salt. (If you are using canned broth, omit the salt.) Turn the heat to high, and bring the liquid to a boil. Cover and cook until the potatoes are fork tender, about 10–20 minutes. Stir in the carrot and the parsley, if you are using it, and cook for an additional minute. Season with salt and pepper to taste.
3. Serve in bowls.

Makes 2–3 servings.

Water

Water is the essential ingredient in most soup. But as late as 1850 only six out of one hundred houses in London had water. Even well-to-do neighborhoods had running water only three times a week! Until the beginning of this century, contaminated water was common, resulting in many deaths from typhoid. Cottagers like Dickon's family were more fortunate. They could rely on fresh water from wells, springs, and rivers.

Pease Pudding

Dried peas, called pease, *were a staple food for cottagers, because they kept well and were cheap and filling. In cottages like Dickon's, almost everything was cooked in a large pot over the fire. Pease pudding—a savory, not a sweet dish— was tied in a cloth and boiled in the pot, often along with salt pork or bacon. The results were like a thick version of what we call split pea soup. Often, once the peas were soft, they were reboiled with eggs and seasonings; sometimes leftover pease pudding was mixed with milk or boiling water to make soup. Serve this pease pudding as you would mashed potatoes, as a side dish with meat.*

Ingredients

lightly salted water
about 1 tablespoon flour
1 pound dried green split peas, rinsed and drained
1 medium onion, chopped
2 pieces of bacon, chopped
1 tablespoon butter
1 teaspoon Worcestershire sauce
salt and pepper to taste

Moor Cure

Cottagers felt a day on the moors among the heather helped cure whooping cough. The windy moors were Dickon's family's cure for many things.

Procedure

1. Bring a large pot of lightly salted water to a boil.
2. Spread out a 1½-foot-square piece of tripled cheesecloth and sprinkle with the flour. Place the split peas in the center. Top with the onion and bacon. Gather up the edges and make a loose sack, making sure the edges are securely tied with a string.
3. Add the pea sack to the boiling water. Cover, and when the water has returned to a boil, reduce the heat to medium-low. Allow the peas to simmer, covered, until very soft, about 1 hour. You may need to add a little water to keep the sack covered.
4. Carefully lift the sack out of the water with tongs and place in a colander to drain for 15 minutes. Untie the string and empty the peas into a bowl. Mix the butter, Worcestershire, and a generous amount of salt and pepper with the peas.
5. Serve warm. If you would like to use the leftovers, as Dickon's family did, reserve some of the cooking water. Combine cooking water and pease pudding to make pea soup.

Makes 4–6 servings.

Pease Pudding Hot

The affordable dried peas cooked into pease pudding, eaten by the poor every-which-way, in droning repetition, inspired this playful rhyme:

*Pease pudding hot!
Pease pudding cold!
Pease pudding
in the pot
Nine days old.*

A variation of the rhyme begins "Pease porridge hot."

Yorkshire Oatcakes

Susan Sowerby, Dickon's mother, would have prepared large quantities of inexpensive oatcakes regularly, cooked on a bakestone suspended from a hook over the fire. Afterward, they were propped up to dry on a block of wood, or even hung up like clothes on a line! Once the oatcakes were firm, Mrs. Sowerby would have stored them for months, or even years, in a wooden chest, buried in oatmeal, so they could be pulled out at any time to heat up for eating.

The greatest luxury was enjoying oatcakes fresh and hot, slathered with butter and sometimes sprinkled with brown sugar. More commonly, they were served broken up in a bowl, like cereal with milk, or eaten like bread, to accompany cheese or sop up gravy or tattie soup.

Ingredients

3½ cups old-fashioned oatmeal
1 cup flour
1 tablespoon sugar (optional)
1 teaspoon salt
1¼ cups warm water, about 105°–115°F.
1 package dry yeast
vegetable oil for frying

Procedure

1. Blend the oatmeal in a food processor or chop until fine. Pour into a large bowl, removing 1½ cups to use later to help shape the oatcakes. Whisk the flour, sugar, and salt into the bowl.
2. Stir the yeast into the water and let sit until dissolved, 3–5 minutes.
3. Pour the yeast-and-water mixture into the oatmeal mixture, stirring until combined. Cover and set aside in a warm, draft-free place to rise for 1 hour.
4. Sprinkle a work surface with the some of the reserved oatmeal. Use a ¼-cup dry measure to scoop out the sticky batter. Turn it out onto the oatmeal-coated surface. Toss and turn the batter in the oatmeal to cover well, using your hands. Slap into a thin oval, about 4 by 2 inches and about ⅓ inch thick, using more oatmeal as needed to prevent sticking. Repeat with the remaining dough to form 9–12 cakes.
5. Preheat the oven to 200°F. Heat 1 tablespoon oil in a large cast-iron skillet over medium heat. Cook the oatcakes in batches, about 3 at a time, adding oil as necessary. Turn when crisp and well browned, about 5 minutes each side. Place the oatcakes on a heat-proof plate in the oven until ready to serve. For best results, cook the oatcakes as you shape them.
6. Serve with butter and brown sugar, or with cheese, or crumbled in milk.

Makes 9–12 oatcakes.

Havercakes

In Yorkshire, oatmeal was far cheaper and more available than flour. So oatcakes, made from ground oatmeal, became a staple food for the working population, including the cottagers like Dickon's family. Oatcakes were also called havercakes in Yorkshire, and were so common that the Yorkshire regiment was called the Havercake Lads. Some say this was because their officers always started a party with an oatcake impaled on their swords!

Cottage Loaf

England's rustic cottage loaf is made from two round loaves, the smaller "topknot" baked on top of the larger ball. Joining the two together may have originally been a way of economizing baking space in a very small oven.

As many cottages had brick ovens, Dickon's mother could have baked cottage loaves weekly in the bottom of the oven. They are a bit tricky to assemble, and not really possible to reproduce exactly because we use electric or gas ovens. Nevertheless, this delicious loaf is reminiscent of a time long gone.

Ingredients

1¼ cups warm water, about 105°–115°F.
¾ teaspoon dry yeast
½ teaspoon sugar
   3 cups bread or all-purpose unbleached white flour (up to ½ cup flour may be replaced by whole wheat flour), plus extra for dusting
1½ teaspoons salt
vegetable oil for coating

Hearth and Range

The kitchen hearth in Dickon's small cottage would probably have been an open or partially enclosed hearth, like a fireplace, with a small oven built into a chimney to one side. It was the center of all household activities. Once the oven fire was lit, it would stay hot enough to bake for twenty-four hours, so on one day each week Mrs. Sowerby made all the bread and other treats, such as parkin, in this oven. In contrast, Misselthwaite Manor probably had a closed

Procedure

1. Combine the water, yeast, and sugar in a small bowl. Allow the mixture to sit until the yeast is dissolved, about 5 minutes.

2. Meanwhile, combine the 3 cups flour and the salt in a large bowl. Add the yeast mixture to the flour and stir until everything is incorporated. Turn out onto a clean surface lightly dusted with flour. Knead, sprinkling on a little additional flour only as necessary to prevent sticking, until the dough becomes smooth and uniform, about 5 minutes.

3. Place the dough in a large bowl that has been lightly coated with vegetable oil. Cover the bowl with a damp cloth or plastic wrap and let the dough rise in a warm, draft-free place, until it is approximately doubled in size, about 1¼ hours.

4. Punch down the dough and cut about a third off for the topknot. Shape both portions into balls and return to the bowl, separating them with plastic wrap so they don't stick together. Cover the bowl with a damp cloth or plastic wrap and let the balls rise again in a warm, draft free place until they are about 50 percent larger, approximately 45 minutes to 1 hour.

5. Preheat the oven to 400°F. Place the bottom ball carefully on a lightly greased baking sheet. Cut a crisscross in the center with a sharp knife and place the smaller ball on top. Press down very gently. Bake for 40–45 minutes, until the top is golden brown and the bottom sounds hollow when tapped. Remove from pan and let cool before slicing.

Makes 1 loaf.

range for cooking, with the fire hidden from view. It would have sat in a large, well-equipped downstairs kitchen, tucked away from the family. It would have been used for baking only, not for heating. Although a great improvement, the Victorian range still had to be lit once a day and had no thermostat, so it took great skill to operate.

Dough-Cakes with Brown Sugar

Stotty cake or oven bottom cakes were often made for a quick meal. Pieces were pulled off the bread dough; they were flattened and baked quickly at the bottom of the oven for 20 minutes, then split and buttered or served with bacon. As there was often plenty of bread dough on hand, cottagers baked small pieces and filled them with brown sugar for a special treat. These days few households make their own bread, but you can use frozen bread or pizza dough that can be found in most supermarkets.

Ingredients

2 teaspoons butter, plus extra for greasing
about 1½ cups cottage loaf dough or frozen bread or
    pizza dough, defrosted and at room temperature
flour for dusting
4 teaspoons dark brown sugar

Procedure

1. Preheat the oven to 400°F.
2. Lightly grease a baking sheet. Divide the dough into four portions. With your hands, pat each portion into a flat disk on the baking sheet, using a little bit of flour only as necessary to keep the dough from sticking.
3. With the dough-cakes on the baking sheet, use a spoon or your thumb to make a slight indentation in the center of each (don't go all the way through!). Drop 1 teaspoonful of brown sugar into each indentation and top it with about ½ teaspoon of butter. Let rest for 15 minutes.
4. Bake the cakes on the bottom of the oven until the dough is browned and cooked through, and the brown sugar and butter are melted. Serve warm.

Makes 4 dough-cakes.

A Cottage Treat

"Martha had even made each of the children a dough-cake with a bit of brown sugar in it."

—The Secret Garden
Chapter 8

There was packaged
food in Mary and
Dickon's day, although
neither probably ate
much of it. This was
fortunate, as most of
the packaged food in
Victorian England
was tainted.

A government inquiry
in 1885 reported that
sulfuric acid was added
to vinegar; coffee was
bulked out with
cornstarch, peas, acorns,
and even plaster of
Paris; and sawdust
was added to cayenne
pepper.

Parkin

*A fine accompaniment to Dickon's tea could have been
a square of this north-country gingerbread, made with
commonly available oatmeal and sticky with treacle, a
relative of molasses. Mrs. Sowerby would have prepared
parkin on baking day and served it throughout the week,
as it gets even better and stickier the longer it sits. Across
Yorkshire, and in the big seaport city of Hull, girls and boys
brought parkin with them to their factory jobs or enjoyed it
at home with a cup of hot tea.*

Ingredients

½ cup butter, plus extra for greasing
1 cup quick or old-fashioned oatmeal
3 cups flour
1 tablespoon ground ginger
1 teaspoon baking soda
1½ teaspoons baking powder
1½ cups dark or light brown sugar
¾ cup treacle or molasses
1 cup milk
1 large egg

Procedure

1. Preheat the oven to 300°F. Grease an 11-by-7-inch baking dish.
2. Blend the oatmeal in a food processor or chop with a knife till fine. Then place it in a large bowl. Sift the flour, ginger, and baking soda and powder together over the oatmeal. Set aside.
3. In a small saucepan melt the brown sugar, treacle or molasses, and ½ cup butter together over medium-low heat, stirring occasionally, about 5 minutes. Remove from the heat. Whisk in the milk, then the egg.
4. Immediately pour the wet mixture into the dry mixture and stir until well combined. Pour into the prepared baking dish, scraping with a rubber spatula to remove it all from the bowl.
5. Bake until just a few crumbs stick to a knife or toothpick that is inserted into the center of the parkin, about 50–60 minutes.
6. Allow the parkin to cool. Remove it from the dish and cut it into squares.

Makes 9–12 squares.

**Parkin and
Guy Fawkes Day**

In Yorkshire parkin was also enjoyed on Guy Fawkes Day, along with baked jacket potatoes and toffee. Guy Fawkes failed in his attempt to blow up King James I and the Houses of Parliament on November 5, 1605. This day is traditionally celebrated with big bonfires that burn his effigy. Everywhere, that is, except at St. Peter's in York, where Fawkes attended school. St. Peter's refuses to burn effigies of past pupils!

"Shut your eyes," said Mary, drawing her footstool closer, "and I will do what my Ayah used to do in India. I will pat your hand and stroke it and sing something quite low."

"I should like that perhaps," Colin said drowsily.

Somehow she was sorry for him and did not want him to lie awake, so she leaned against the bed and began to stroke and pat his hand and sing a very low little chanting song in Hindustani.

"That is nice," he said more drowsily still, and she went on chanting and stroking, but when she looked at him again his black lashes were lying close against his cheeks, for his eyes were shut and he was fast asleep. So she got up softly, took her candle and crept away without making a sound.

—The Secret Garden
Chapter 14

A Taste of India

Fruit Lassi
Sooji
Little Bacon and Coriander Pancakes
Fresh Mango Chutney
Mulligatawny Soup
Florence Nightingale's Kedgeree

Children of the Raj

Mary's female attendant, her Ayah, and other servants of the house waited on Mary for everything; she didn't even dress herself. Most likely as a toddler she was carried by a servant in a large wicker backpack, while another walked behind her, holding a parasol above to protect her pale skin from the harsh Indian sun. At bedtime Mary's Ayah probably tucked her into a cocoon of mosquito netting. When Mary was older, her parents probably would have

A Taste of India

India was very different from Mary's new home at Misselthwaite Manor. A battery of servants, including her nursemaid—her Ayah—waited on her constantly. But what was Mary doing in India? India and England's relationship goes back 400 years, to when England started to colonialize India to control the spice trade. By Mary's time England's hold on India was complete, with Queen Victoria named Empress of India. This was the height of the "British Raj," the name for the colonial English world in India.

Many British soldiers, merchants, and diplomats lived in India during the Victorian Era and created an exclusive enclave for themselves, often at the expense of the native Indians. The English built railroads, bridges, and canals, but they did so with the labor of grossly underpaid Indians. And as Mary's own behavior illustrates, this British ruling class often treated natives as conquered inferiors.

Most of the British in India were middle class, but they were able to live (and dine) more lavishly than in England because of the large pool of native servants. A native cook was essential to this army of local servants. Through long apprenticeship Indian cooks learned to cook English foods, toning down the exotic, aromatic, and often highly spiced Indian foods to suit the more timid English palate. This combining of Indian and English foods is called *Anglo-Indian*. Mary would have eaten such food in India, and it also became quite popular in England itself during the Victorian Era.

As in England, British children in India usually had their main meal, lunch, in the nursery. This midday meal, called "tiffin," was a welcome break from a hot day and was often followed by a nap. A basic tiffin included salads, curries, leftover roasts with relishes and pickles, and for dessert ice creams, fruit fools, and jellies.

Mary's mother may have socialized with friends at a more elegant tiffin, taken a nap, and then gone on a late-afternoon inspection of the gardens. After a bath and tea, she might have dressed for a promenade and finished off the day with an elaborate dinner, served by bearers. In fact, at the end of the nineteenth century, during Mary's time in India, dinners became grandiose, with cooks going to such great lengths to disguise the food in a variety of fancy forms that some food writers made pleas for simpler dishes.

sent her back to England to be schooled, partly to protect her from tropical fevers and scorpion and snake bites. (The Secret Garden talks of Mary's yellow skin, which may have resulted from jaundice.) In fact the English officer's wife who accompanied Mary back to England was taking her children "home" to boarding school.

The Hot Season

Like the majority of the English, Mary's family would have based their rhythms around India's intense seasons—hot, cool, and rainy. When the hot season came, everyone was sapped of energy. But to escape the fierce heat, many English went to the colder "hills," as the Himalayan Mountains were called.

"The hills" were piney and cooler, and life was more casual and slow paced there. Picnics were popular with families of the British Raj, with

Fruit Lassi

A lassi is a cool yogurt shake made with fresh fruit. Such a drink may have helped Mary cool off during the sweltering hot seasons in India.

Ingredients

For Mango Lassi:
1 ripe mango
8 ounces plain yogurt
½ cup milk
⅛ teaspoon ground cinnamon
1 pinch ground cumin (optional)
1–2 tablespoons honey, to taste

For Peach Lassi:
1 can (15 ounces) of sliced peaches in pear juice
8 ounces plain yogurt
⅛ teaspoon ground cinnamon
1 pinch ground cumin (optional)
1–2 tablespoons honey, to taste

Procedure

To make Mango Lassi:

1. Stand the mango on its small end. To remove the flesh from the pit, use a sharp knife to cut the fruit vertically, sliding the knife along the pit on one side. Repeat on the other side, which will give you two large pieces. Then scoop out the meat and discard the peel.
2. Combine the mango flesh in a blender or food processor with the yogurt, milk, cinnamon, and cumin if you are using it, and blend until smooth.
3. Add honey until you reach the desired sweetness and blend again. Serve as is or over ice, or, if you prefer, chill for an hour before serving.

To make Peach Lassi:
Proceed from #2, omitting the milk.

Serves 2–3.

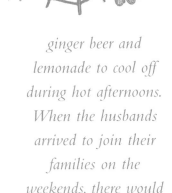

ginger beer and lemonade to cool off during hot afternoons. When the husbands arrived to join their families on the weekends, there would be dinner parties and more festivities.

The Social Season

*The "winter" season
in India is sunny and
dry, and cooler to
cold depending on
the location. This
relatively comfortable
weather was the big
social season for the
British Raj, a time of
luncheon and dinner
parties, hunting and
riding, evening
costume masquerades,
afternoon teas and
cricket matches,
and courting.
As India was a
military outpost, there
were more English
men than women.
Still, the marriage
rules for a soldier were
strict. He couldn't even*

Sooji

Indian winters can be cold, especially with the lack of central heating and the contrast to the scalding summers. Alone in her nursery on a chilly morning, Mary might have warmed up with this breakfast cereal, not unlike cream of wheat. Sooji gets its lovely nutty flavor from toasting the semolina, which is a variety of wheat also used in some Indian sweets. Semolina can be purchased in health or specialty food stores.

Ingredients

⅓ cup semolina
2 cups water
pinch of salt

Procedure

1. Put the semolina into a small, heavy saucepan or medium skillet. Heat over medium heat, stirring frequently, until it smells toasted and turns a very light brown, about 5–7 minutes.
2. Stir in the water and salt and whisk to combine. Simmer, stirring frequently, until thickened, about 3–5 minutes.
3. Pour the sooji into bowls and top with brown sugar and milk to taste.

Makes 2–3 servings.

become engaged until he was thirty years old and his fiancée had been approved by his senior officer. Even then, engagements had to last a full year. Nevertheless, many marriageable ladies sailed for India during the social season. If they didn't make a match, they went home to England, where they were cruelly called "returned empties."

Breakfast in India

Most likely Mary's household rose before dawn, as in the hot season it was sweltering by ten A.M. "Chota-bazri," or early tea, would be brought on trays by servants to the bedrooms. Afterward, Mary's mother might have enjoyed an early horseback ride and bath before a hearty breakfast, which could have included kedgeree, eggs, and hot chocolate.

Little Bacon and Coriander Pancakes

English bacon and Indian seasonings are added to pancakes, lending an exotic taste to a simple dish. This recipe was adapted from Jennifer Brennans's wonderful memoirs of British life in India, Curries and Bugles. *Serve these as part of an Anglo-Indian tea or breakfast.*

Ingredients

½ cup flour
1 egg
½ cup milk
1 tablespoon chopped coriander leaves (also called cilantro)
1 teaspoon curry powder
2 slices bacon, chopped
3 tablespoons mango chutney

Procedure

1. Place the flour in a medium bowl. Whisk in the egg, milk, coriander, and curry powder until the mixture forms a well-combined batter. Set aside.
2. Cook the bacon in a large cast-iron or nonstick skillet over medium heat, stirring frequently. When it is crisp, about 5 minutes, remove with a slotted spoon and place on a paper towel. Discard the fat, leaving a thin coat in the skillet for the pancakes to cook in.
3. Preheat the oven to 200°F. Heat the skillet over medium heat. Crumble the bacon. Add pancake batter 1 tablespoon at a time. Leave room between spoonfuls for the batter to spread. Immediately sprinkle each pancake with a pinch of the bacon. At this point they should be slightly brown and ready to turn. Cook until the second side browns slightly, about 30 seconds. Remove the pancakes to a plate and place in the oven. Finish making the pancakes with the rest of the batter.
4. Briefly warm the chutney on the stove or in the microwave, about 1 minute.
5. Place the warm pancakes on plates, and top each with a little mango chutney. Eat immediately.

Makes about 16 little pancakes.

A sprig of cilantro

One Endless Breakfast

Generally, as the nineteenth century wore on, breakfasts got simpler, but as late as 1900, one Englishwoman described an elaborate Indian breakfast that started with mulligatawny soup and ended, fourteen courses later, with ice cream!

Fresh Mango Chutney

Chutney is a fruit condiment, used traditionally to accompany curries, which are hot and spicy Indian dishes. But it is also used to zip up plainer dishes like bacon and coriander pancakes or roasted chicken.

Chutney gets its name from the Indian word chatni *and its sweet-and-sour taste from fruit and vinegar. A wide variety of chutneys became popular in England during Queen Victoria's reign. The British created very sweet bottled chutneys, which are close to their beloved fruit preserves.*

Ingredients

1 ripe mango
2 tablespoons water
1 teaspoon grated ginger
pinch of hot pepper flakes (optional)
2 tablespoons raisins
1 tablespoon cider vinegar

Procedure

1. Stand the mango on its small end. To remove the flesh from the pit, use a sharp knife to cut the fruit vertically, sliding the knife along the pit on one side. Repeat on the other side, which will give you two large pieces. Then scoop out the meat and discard the peel.
2. Put half the mango into a small pot, along with the water, ginger, and hot pepper, if you are using it. Cook, covered, over medium–low heat, until the mango pieces start to fall apart, about 5 minutes.
3. Remove from the heat and stir in the remaining mango, raisins, and vinegar. Set aside until ready to usc. If you are not using the mango chutney until the following day, add the vinegar just before serving.

Makes about ¾ cup.

Shawls, idols, durbars,
*   brandy-pawny;*
Rupees, clever
*   jugglers, dust-storms,*
*   slipper'd feet,*
Rainy season, and
*   mulligatawny.*

*   —From "Curry &*
Rice," on Forty Plates
*   by George Francklin*
*   Atkinson, 1859*

Indian Spices

To get a feeling for the aromas of Mary's early life in India, try mulligatawny soup or kedgeree, which include just a few of the many spices used in Indian cooking. Some, like cinnamon, cloves, ginger, and nutmeg, made their way into the English diet long ago. But many others, like cardamom and fenugreek, remain exotic to the British (and Americans) even today. Curry powder, the most famous Indian seasoning, is not an individual spice but a combination of

Mulligatawny Soup

This golden soup was created two centuries ago in southern India by local cooks for the English. Mulligatawny *means "pepper water," so named for the slightly spicy flavor it derives from curry.*

Like many Anglo-Indian dishes, mulligatawny was quite fashionable during the Victorian Era, the height of England's hold on India.

Ingredients

½ cup rice and lightly salted water (or 1 cup leftover cooked rice)
2 tablespoons butter
2½ tablespoons flour
2 teaspoons curry
1 garlic clove, minced
⅓ cup water
1 can (13¾ ounces) reduced-sodium chicken broth
1 skinless and boneless chicken breast, cut into small cubes
⅔ cup coconut milk, plus extra for garnish
2 teaspoons fresh lemon juice

Procedure

1. (If you are using leftover rice, skip this step.) Put the rice into a medium pot of rapidly boiling lightly salted water and boil until tender, 18–20 minutes. Drain and set aside.
2. While the rice is cooking, melt the butter in a medium pot over medium-low heat. Stir in the flour and continue stirring until it smells like a pie crust but doesn't brown, 2–5 minutes. Add the curry and garlic and stir to combine.
3. Whisk in the ⅓ cup water thoroughly to remove the lumps, then stir in the broth and chicken. Cook over medium-low heat, until the soup is thickened and the chicken just cooked through, 3–5 minutes.
4. Stir in the coconut milk and cook, but do not boil. Stir in the lemon juice.
5. Divide the soup equally among four shallow bowls. Place ¼ cup rice in the center of each bowl. If you wish, it is pretty to drizzle the soup with a little extra coconut milk and a sprinkling of cilantro. Serve immediately.

up to twenty freshly ground spices combined in a wide variety of ways. Packaged preground curry powder became popular in England during the Victorian Era.

Makes 4 servings.

Florence Nightingale's Kedgeree

Naming dishes after famous people, such as the well-known nurse Florence Nightingale, was a popular practice in Victorian times, even if they had nothing to do with the dish.

Kedgeree was commonly served for both breakfast and lunch, as it was an excellent way to use leftover fish and rice. It is an English version of the Indian dish khichiri, *made with rice and spiced lentils. Khichiri can be prepared with fish and yellow-colored turmeric rice seasoned with chilis, fresh ginger, and fried onions. The milder English kedgeree, also called "breakfast rice," is surprisingly satisfying and is a delicious way to start the day. It is still popular in England today.*

Ingredients

¾ cup white rice
lightly salted water
2 eggs
1 tablespoon butter, plus extra for the toast
6–8 ounces smoked haddock or trout, skinned,
    bones removed, and flaked
pinch of pepper (optional)
pinch of nutmeg (optional)
1–2 tablespoons freshly grated Parmesan cheese
2 slices of bread, crusts removed

Procedure

1. Put the rice into a medium pot of rapidly boiling lightly salted water and boil it until tender, 18–20 minutes. Drain in a colander.
2. While the rice is cooking, put the eggs in a small pot and cover with water by an inch. Bring to a boil, then reduce to a low simmer and cook for 10–15 minutes. Drain, run under cold water, and peel. Separate the whites and yolks and with a wooden spoon press the yolks and whites separately through a sieve. Set aside.
3. Melt 1 tablespoon butter in a pot. Add the cooked rice, flaked fish, and pepper and nutmeg, if you are using them. Very gently stir over low heat until warm and well combined. Stir in the sieved egg whites.
4. On a small platter, pile up the kedgeree. Sprinkle the sieved egg yolks and Parmesan cheese over the top. Toast the bread and butter it. Cut each slice into four triangles and surround the kedgeree with the buttered toast. Serve warm or at room temperature.

Serves 4.

A stalk of rice

The Queen and Her Curry

Indian dishes became quite popular during Victoria's reign, and it is no wonder, as the contrast with the mild food of England must have been refreshing. The Queen herself enjoyed curries cooked by Abdul Karim, her Indian Groom of the Chamber. He also taught her a few words of Hindi.

From that time the exercises were part of the day's duties as much as the Magic was. It became possible for both Colin and Mary to do more of them each time they tried, and such appetites were the results that but for the basket Dickon put down behind the bush each morning when he arrived they would have been lost. But the little oven in the hollow and Mrs. Sowerby's bounties were so satisfying that Mrs. Medlock and the nurse and Dr. Craven became mystified again. You can trifle with your breakfast and seem to disdain your dinner if you are full to the brim with roasted eggs and potatoes and richly frothed new milk and oat-cakes and buns and heather honey and clotted cream.

—The Secret Garden
Chapter 24

Garden Picnics

Roasted Potatoes and Eggs

Currant Buns

Crumpets

Cornish Pasties

Chocolate Picnic Biscuits

A Victorian Picnic

The ideal period picnic is described by popular Victorian cookbook author Mrs. Beeton. Keep in mind that her suggested menu is for forty people!

"A joint of cold roast beef, a joint of cold boiled beef, 2 ribs of lamb, 2 shoulders of lamb, 4 roast fowls, 2 roast ducks, 1 ham, 1 tongue, 2 veal and ham pies, 6 medium-sized lobsters, 1 epic of collared calf's head, 4 quartern loaves of household bread, 3 dozen rolls, 6 loaves of tin bread (for tea), 2 plain plum cakes,

Garden Picnics

In a secret garden with good friends, food tastes glorious. Or so Mary and Dickon felt when they savored their simple garden picnics of smoky potatoes and eggs, roasted in an improvised oven, and currant buns, cottage loaf, and fresh milk.

From rustic to ornate, picnics were extremely popular in Victorian England, despite the region's tendency to be damp and drizzly. Children's parties, hunting expeditions, or family get-togethers were all fine occasions for a picnic.

Picnics were held in a variety of settings. For the wealthy, they often included journeys into attractive landscapes. At a fashionable picnic, the ladies might sketch the scenery while the gentlemen looked for archaeological remains or wild mushrooms.

One of the most popular picnics in a natural setting would take place on a day of game shooting and was called a shooting party. The meals were elaborate and might include game pies, hams, beef pudding, potatoes in their jackets, and Irish stew, finished off with a few desserts, such as plum pudding or mince pies. Food would be served, when weather allowed, on trestle tables laid with linen by a butler.

One turn-of-the-century children's picnic was an

end-of-the-year tea for a children's school. This lawn picnic, given by the Marquis and Marchioness of Bristol, was held at a great mansion. Beforehand, the children were given a talk on what was expected of them: They were to be impeccably clean and tidy, to speak quietly, to keep with partners, and not to walk in cowpats, of which there were many. The lord and lady were waiting for them on the lawn, and the children were supposed to say good afternoon and the girls to curtsy and boys to bow.

When she heard the protocol, one girl's grandmother commanded her not curtsy, because she felt no one was better than her granddaughter. Terrified of flouting convention, the girl took refuge in the pigsty. Luckily, when she emerged, there were too many children to be presented anyway. The children simply called good afternoon to their host and hostess and raced to the food.

The picnic itself was laid out on long tables set under the trees, piled high with mountains of bread and butter, slices of fruit cake, and plenty of iced sponge cake, which was so popular that the youngest children didn't get any.

2 pound cakes, 2 sponge cakes, a tin of mixed biscuits, ½ lb. of tea. Coffee is not suitable for a picnic, being difficult to make."

—Mrs. Beeton's Book of Household Management, *1909*

Roasted Potatoes and Eggs

Improvising an oven wouldn't have been a difficult thing for Dickon to do, as he was a handy child and may have watched his mother cook in an open hearth in their cottage.

For the contemporary cook an oven can be created in a fireplace or charcoal grill. The results are the same, and you will feel the sense of wonder, as Mary and Colin did, when you picnic on this delicious smoky-flavored food.

Ingredients

4 eggs
4 medium new potatoes, scrubbed and
   cut into quarters
4 pats of butter
salt and pepper to taste

Procedure

1. Make a charcoal fire in a grill or fireplace.
2. While the fire is heating up, wrap each egg in foil. Then, on a piece of foil, place a quartered potato; top with a pat of butter, and salt and pepper to taste. Wrap the foil loosely around the potato, and seal tightly. Repeat with the remaining potatoes, butter, salt, and pepper.
3. When the coals are completely gray and have started to turn to ash a little, carefully nestle the potatoes among them, using long tongs. In 10 minutes add the eggs off to the side where it is a little cooler, but still touching the coals. In another 10 minutes use the tongs to carefully remove the eggs and one potato packet.
4. Open the potato packet. You should be able to easily pierce the potato with a fork, but "hearth" cooking is more variable than oven cooking. If it is still slightly hard, return the packet to the coals for an additional 5–10 minutes. When the potatoes are done, carefully remove them all from the fire.
5. As soon as you can handle them, open the egg and potato packets and enjoy.

Makes 4 servings.

A potato plant

A Secret Picnic

"Dickon made the stimulating discovery that in the wood in the park outside the garden where Mary had first found him piping to the wild creatures there was a deep little hollow where you could build a sort of tiny oven with stones and roast potatoes and eggs in it."

—The Secret Garden
Chapter 24

117

Currants

*So many dried
currants were used in
Victorian baking that
the entire Greek crop
was absorbed by the
English market.
Dickon's mother
would have bought
currants in bulk. Then
she picked out bits of
grit and soil, and even
flies. After that the
currants had to be
washed, dried by the
fire, and warmed
before baking. Arduous
though this sounds, it
didn't stop the English
from consuming
millions of pounds
annually.*

Currant Buns

*These are dense yeast-risen buns, perfumed with a touch of
spice and packed with sweet currants. Spiced buns, often
sweetened with dried currants, became popular in England
during the Tudor period. For a long time the law decreed
that they could be prepared by bakers only on special
occasions, like Good Friday and Christmas. So those who
craved them more frequently had to bake buns at home. Still
warm from the cottage chimney oven and accompanied by
milk, these buns made the ideal picnic treat.*

Ingredients

Buns
1¼ cups milk
¼ cup brown sugar
4 tablespoons butter, plus extra for greasing
4 cups flour, plus extra for kneading
1 teaspoon cinnamon
½ teaspoon ground nutmeg
generous pinch of salt
1 package yeast
1 large egg
⅔ cup dried
   currants

Glaze
milk
sugar

Procedure

1. Warm the milk, sugar, and 4 tablespoons butter in a small pot until the butter is melted and the mixture is about the temperature of bathwater (105°–115°F.). Do not let boil.
2. While the milk mixture is heating, measure the 4 cups flour, cinnamon, nutmeg, and salt into a large bowl and put the yeast into a small bowl.
3. When the milk mixture reaches the right temperature, add about ¼ cup of the liquid to the yeast and stir with a fork. Let sit to dissolve the yeast, about 3–5 minutes.
4. Add the yeast mixture to the center of the flour. Drop the egg into the rest of the milk mixture, stir to combine, and immediately add on top of the flour. Stir in the currants and mix the dough with your hands, then knead on a lightly floured board until the dough is rubbery, about 5 minutes.
5. Lightly cover with a damp cloth or plastic wrap and let sit in a warm place until doubled in size, about 1¼–3 hours.
6. Cut the dough in half, then quarters, then each quarter in fours again. Shape into 16 rounds. Place on one or two lightly greased baking sheets, with the buns almost touching. Let rise for 30 minutes to 1 hour until doubled in bulk. Preheat the oven to 400°F.
7. Brush the tops of the buns with milk. Sprinkle each with sugar.
8. Bake until the buns are browned and cooked all the way through, about 15–25 minutes.

Makes 16 buns.

A currant grape vine

Mell Cakes

Like Dickon's beloved currant buns, mell cakes were made with currants. Mell means the last of the harvest, and the custom was that those who helped with a farmer's harvest would be rewarded with a mell supper and barn dance. Mell cakes were eaten during the festivities, and the last sheaf of corn to be harvested was tied up with flowers and ribbons and known as the "mell sheaf" or "mell doll."

Picnic Crumpets

Because they are best when eaten warm, crumpets are almost always served indoors, with tea. Perhaps Mary and Colin managed to toast their crumpets over an open fire and spread them with fresh creamy butter from Mrs. Sowerby.

"When the white cloth was spread upon the grass, with hot tea and buttered toast and crumpets, a delightfully hungry meal was eaten."

—The Secret Garden
Chapter 24

Crumpets

Crumpets are related to what we call the English muffin, but are even softer in the middle. They are a bit tricky to make and require a "crumpet ring," which measures about 3 inches in diameter and 2 inches high. If you don't have rings, try a metal cookie cutter of any size. Be sure to have a metal spatula and tongs on hand to turn the crumpets and lift off the rings.

Ingredients

2 cups flour
¼ teaspoon salt
1 cup milk
1 tablespoon vegetable oil, plus extra to cook with
1 teaspoon sugar
1 package dried yeast
½ cup warm water, plus extra if needed
butter for spreading

Procedure

1. Measure the flour and salt into a large mixing bowl and place in a warm spot.
2. Warm the milk, 1 tablespoon oil, and sugar in a small pan to about the temperature of bathwater (105°–115°F.). Remove from the heat. Pour about 3 tablespoons of the milk mixture into a small bowl. Whisk in the package of yeast. Pour this liquid and the remaining milk mixture into the bowl with the flour. Combine thoroughly with a wooden spoon and continue to beat for about 5 minutes.
3. Cover the batter and allow it to rise in a warm place for 1–1½ hours.
4. Add the ½ cup warm water to the dough, then stir until thoroughly combined. Cover again and let rest in a warm place for ½ hour.
5. Heat a large cast-iron skillet on medium-high heat. Place about 1 tablespoon of oil in the skillet. Thoroughly oil the rings and add as many rings as will comfortably fit in the pan but still allow you to turn the rings. Carefully spoon the batter into one ring until it fills ½ to ⅔ up the sides. Watch carefully to see if bubbles appear on top in 2–5 minutes. If they do, continue filling the remaining rings. If not, beat up to ¼ cup more warm water into the batter and try again.
6. When all the rings are filled and the tops start to become solid, about 10 minutes, remove each ring, beginning with the first you filled, and cook the crumpet on the other side for another 10 minutes.
7. When the crumpets are cooked, spread them with butter and toast them in a preheated broiler until they are crisp.

Makes 12–15 crumpets.

Crumpet Toaster

Crumpets are yeasty muffins that are full of holes. They are often toasted by the fire during teatime; Victorian children would sometimes fight for the privilege of being the official crumpet toaster!

**Shooting Party
Picnic**

*A popular adult picnic
was known as a
shooting party picnic.
After a morning of
shooting, the ladies
and gentlemen would
eat, while loaders
would partake
separately. Of course,
not all the game could
be consumed, so much
of the game was sent
to friends or to local
merchants to sell,
often by the mail.
One pheasant was
misaddressed, could
not be delivered, and
was returned several
weeks later. Needless
to say, the bird was
rather ripe!*

Cornish Pasties

*Cold meat pies are typical of English cooking. Meat turnovers,
called pasties, are a favorite. As everyone in the family liked
to season pasties in his or her own way, it become the custom
to mark the corner of the pasty with one's initials.*

*Cornish pasties originated in Cornwall, the peninsula that
is southwestern England. They made an ideal portable lunch
or picnic item for the working class. Although often filled with
meat, in hard times potatoes were used, and the resulting
pasties were called tiddy oggies, because* tiddy *is the Cornish
name for potato. Sweet fillings, such as clove-spiced apples or,
as in Yorkshire, raisins and fresh mint were also popular.*

Ingredients

Crust
3 cups flour, plus extra for dusting
1 teaspoon salt
8 ounces lard (½ block) or butter, cut into
    small pieces
½ cup plus 1 tablespoon water

Filling
½ pound beef chuck, cut into 1-inch cubes
1 small onion, quartered
1 small turnip, peeled and quartered
1 small new potato, cut into 8 pieces
1 teaspoon salt, or to taste
¼ teaspoon pepper
¼ teaspoon dried thyme, optional

Glaze
1 egg
2 teaspoons water

Procedure

1. Place the 3 cups flour, salt, and lard in a food processor. Pulse until coarsely chopped. Pour in the water and pulse two or three times, until just combined. You can also make dough using a pastry cutter or fork.

2. Turn the dough out onto a lightly floured board and divide into quarters. Form each quarter into a ball and roll it out with a rolling pin until it is a little larger than a saucer. Place a saucer on top of one quarter and trim around the saucer. Repeat to make four circles of dough. Discard the extra dough.

3. One at a time, pulse the beef, onion, turnip, and potato until finely chopped, emptying the food processor into the same bowl after each operation. Add the salt and pepper, and the thyme, if you are using it. You can also chop all the ingredients by hand.

4. Preheat the oven to 425°F. Place one quarter of the filling in the center of each round of pastry dough. Fold in half to make a semicircle, and seal the edges. Mix the egg and water in a bowl and brush the tops with this glaze.

5. Place the pasties on an ungreased baking sheet and bake for 20 minutes. Reduce the heat to 350°F., and bake until well browned, another 30–35 minutes. (If the glaze starts to get too dark, cover the top loosely with foil.) Serve warm or at room temperature.

Makes 4 pasties.

Picnics in a Damp Climate

"A picnic is the Englishman's grand gesture, his final defiance flung in the face of faith. . . . [He] refuses to frequent an outdoor cafe of any sort, obstinately clinging to his picnic basket and wet and wasp-haunted field."

—*Georgina Battiscombe,* English Picnics, *1949*

Chocolate Picnic Biscuits

Before the nineteenth century, homemade biscuits (or cookies, as we call them) were the norm. But the increased technology and factory labor of the industrial revolution brought many convenience foods, such as packaged biscuits and tins of cocoa powder, into the stores. People quickly learned to combine commercial products to create new dishes, like these quickly assembled picnic biscuits.

You can find tea biscuits in the cookie section of your supermarket.

Ingredients

1 package (7 ounces) rich tea or any English
   sweet biscuit
7 tablespoons sweet butter
¼ cup dark corn syrup or English "golden syrup"
3 tablespoons cocoa powder
2 tablespoons sugar

Sugar

Victorian recipes often call for pounded sugar, because sugar came in the form of conical loaves about 15 inches high, which were sold whole or broken up into chunks by the grocer. At home, pieces were pounded with a rolling pin or a bottle and sieved to make a fine powder.

Procedure

1. Put the biscuits in a plastic bag inside a paper bag. Seal well and pound with a rolling pin or can until they are broken up into small pieces.
2. Combine the butter, syrup, cocoa powder, and sugar in a small saucepan. Heat over medium heat, just until the butter is melted, whisking together to thoroughly combine. Remove from the heat. Stir in the biscuit pieces.
3. Lay the crumbly mixture on a large sheet of waxed paper. Loosely mold it into a log shape, then roll it up in the paper. Chill for at least 1 hour, and up to 3 days.
4. Cut with a serrated knife into rounds. Alternatively, the dough can be pressed into an 8-inch square baking dish, chilled, and cut into "fingers."

Makes 18–20 biscuits or fingers.

A Picnic Poem

If polar bears were everywheres,

and leopards came to tea,

And fearful bats and gnawing gnats

all came to eat with me,

And giant snakes ate all the cakes,

What a "picnic" that would be!

—*Jane Eayre,* The Mary Frances Cook Book, *1914*

Index

Items in *italics* refer to recipe titles.

A

Apricot Fool, 70–71

B

bacon, 17, 20, 84, 86
    and coriander pancakes, little,
        104–5, 106
baking powder, 53
"bangers," 24
beef, 31, 83, 114, 122, 123
    tea, 48
berries, 16, 56, 63, 68, 69, 70, 72, 73, 74,
        75, 78, 79, 83
bilberries, 16, 83
biscuits, 31, 115
Brandy Snap Baskets with Whipped Cream,
        58–59
bread, 31, 47, 92, 114, 115
    cottage loaf, 90–91
    in dough-cakes with brown
        sugar, 92, 93
    in summer pudding, 68-69
Bread Sauce, 34–35

C

Cabinet Pudding, 31, 40–41
cakes, 30, 51, 52, 114, 115
    dough, with brown sugar, 92–93
    fruit tea loaf, 54–55
carrots, glazed, 66–67
cheddar cheese, 22, 23, 38, 39
cheese, 20, 22, 23, 31, 38, 39, 82, 88
Cheese Muffins, 22–23
chicken, 30, 34, 35, 37, 106, 108, 109

chocolate, hot. *See Cocoa*
Chocolate Picnic Biscuits, 124–25
chutney, fresh mango, 106–7
clotted cream, 53, 78
Cocoa, 17, 26–27, 104
cocoa powder, 26, 27, 124, 125
Coddled Eggs, 20–21
coffee, 17, 94, 115
Cornish Pasties, 122–23
Cottage Loaf, 83, 90–91
Cranberry Fool, 70–71
Crumpets, 17, 120–21
Cucumber Tea Sandwiches, 50–51
Currant Buns, 83, 118–19
currants, 18, 52, 118, 119
curry, 106, 108, 111
custard sauce, 42
"cut and come again cake," 54

D

Dough-Cakes with Brown Sugar, 10, 92–93
drippings, 31, 83, 84

E

eggs, 17, 27, 48, 104
    coddled, 20–21
    roasted potatoes and, 116–17

F

fish, 30, 77, 110, 111
Florence Nightingale's Kedgeree, 110–11
fools, 99
    apricot, 70–71
    cranberry, 70–71
fowl, 83, 114, 122. *See also* chicken
    roasted, with bread sauce, 34–35

Fresh Mango Chutney, 106–7
Fresh Spring Peas with Mint, 64–65
fruit, 30, 37, 40, 62, 63, 68, 70, 74, 76, 78, 82
Fruit Lassi, 100–101
Fruit Tea Loaf, 54–55

G

garden, 62–63, 70, 72
ginger, 59
Glazed Carrots, 30, 66–67

H

herbs, 62, 63, 70, 71. *See also* sage, mint
honey, 83
hot chocolate. *See Cocoa*

I

ice, 76, 77

J

jam, 47, 48, 52
    raspberry, 72-73
    sauce, 42
Jam Roly Poly, 42–43
jelly roll tea spiral, 50

K

kedgeree, 104, 108
    Florence Nightingale's, 110–11
kidneys, 17
koumiss, 48

L

lassi, 100–101
Lemon Curd Tartlettes, 56–57
Little Bacon and Coriander Pancakes, 104–5, 106
Little Sausage Cakes, 20, 24–25

M

malt liquor, home-brewed, 48
mango
    chutney, 106–7
    lassi, 100–101
meats, 17, 30, 31, 32, 34, 39, 47, 82, 84, 99, 114. *See also* beef, chicken, fish, fowl, mutton, pork
mell cakes, 119
mint, 64, 65
Molded Spiced Pears, 31, 76–77
muffins, cheese, 22–23
Mulligatawny Soup, 105, 108–9
mutton, 17

O

oatcakes, Yorkshire, 88–89
oatmeal, 88, 89
oats, 18, 19

P

pancakes, little bacon and coriander, 104–5, 106
Parkin, 83, 94–95
pasties, 116
    Cornish, 122–23
peach lassi, 100–101
pears, molded spiced, 31, 76–77
peas
    fresh spring, with mint, 64–65
    split, 86, 87
Pease Pudding, 86–87
pork, 24
Porridge, 10, 12, 16, 18–19, 30, 36
    pease, 83, 87. *See also Pease Pudding*
potatoes, 10, 30, 31, 36, 83, 84, 85, 114, 122
    in potato snow, 36–37

potatoes *(cont.)*
    roasted, and eggs, 114, 116–17
    in tattie broth, 83, 84–85
Potato Snow, 30, 36–37
Proper Pot of Tea, A, 48–49
pudding, 30, 40, 42, 47, 84
    cabinet, 31, 40–41
    Christmas, 41
    jam roly poly, 42–43
    pease, 86–87
    plum, 83, 114
    rice or suet, 40
    summer, 68–69
    Yorkshire, 32–33

Q

Queen Anne's lace (wild carrots), 66

R

rabbit, fried, 17
raisins, 18, 40, 54
raspberries, 68, 69, 72, 74
Raspberry Jam, 72–73, 76
Raspberry Vinegar, 74–75
rice, 108, 109, 110, 111
Roasted Fowl with Bread Sauce, 30, 34–35,
    106
Roasted Potatoes and Eggs, 116–17

S

sage, 24, 25
sandwiches, 50, 51
    cucumber tea, 50–51
sausage, 24
sausage cakes, little, 20, 24–25
Scones, 17, 52–53
"slow walking bread," 54
Sooji, 102–3

soup, 30, 84
    mulligatawny, 108–9
    tattie broth, 83, 84–85, 88
spices, 59, 98–99, 108, 109
split peas, green, 86, 87
Strawberries and Cream, 78–79
sugar, 124
Summer Pudding, 68–69

T

tartlettes, lemon curd, 56–57
Tattie Broth, 83, 84–85, 88
tea, 17, 46–47, 49, 54, 55, 115, 120
    a proper pot of, 48–49
tea sandwiches, 50, 51
toad-in-the-hole, 33
toast, 20
treacle, 18, 94
Two Fools, 70–71

V

vegetables, 30, 31, 47, 62, 63, 65, 66, 67,
    69, 82, 83, 84, 92, 99. *See also*
    carrots, peas, potatoes
vinegar, 94
    raspberry, 74–75

W

water, 85
Welsh Rabbit, 38–39

Y

yeast, 53
yogurt, 100, 101
Yorkshire Oatcakes, 88–89
Yorkshire Pudding, 32–33